THE DELECTABLE TART

MERRY FARMER

THE DELECTABLE TART

Copyright ©2019 by Merry Farmer

This ebook is licensed for your personal enjoyment only. This ebook may not be re-sold or given away to other people. If you would like to share this book with another person, please purchase an additional copy for each recipient. If you're reading this book and did not purchase it, or it was not purchased for your use only, then please return to your digital retailer and purchase your own copy. Thank you for respecting the hard work of this author.

This book is a work of fiction. Names, characters, places, and incidents are products of the author's imagination or are used fictitiously. Any resemblance to actual events or locales or persons, living or dead, is entirely coincidental.

Cover design by Erin Dameron-Hill (the miracle-worker)

ASIN: B07MB7X7TT

Paperback ISBN: 9781793005984

Click here for a complete list of other works by Merry Farmer.

If you'd like to be the first to learn about when the next books in the series come out and more, please sign up for my newsletter here:
http://eepurl.com/RQ-KX

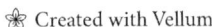 Created with Vellum

For Rachel...
Or maybe I should say Andrew...
Who has definitely enjoyed beta-reading these books!

CHAPTER 1

LONDON – 1815

*I*t wasn't fair. Sophie Barnes stood to one side of the grand parlor in her brother-in-law, the Marquess of Landsbury's, London townhome, watching the odd assortment of friends that her sisters had made over the last two months laughing, chattering, and congratulating her sister Honor on her marriage to wealthy merchant, Sebastian Boothe. Sophie stood with shoulders slouched, feeling as close to miserable as it was possible to feel in such merry company.

They weren't her friends, though she found the assortment of courtesans, actors, and *nouveau riche* fascinating. The scandalous gowns that the women wore, along with a glittering array of paste jewels—and real gems as well, in a few cases—wasn't the sedate and respectable style she was used to. The men were far too informal, compared to the stiff, polite gentlemen she had spent her life associating with. Several of Honor and Sebastian's guests were gentlemen she knew, at least by name, who had been invited by their mistresses. But the manner in which they behaved was so inconsistent with everything Sophie knew as to make them appear to be different people entirely.

Sophie's friends were a different sort altogether. Except that they were no longer her friends. Ever since The Disaster at Almack's, when her sister Verity had made an inopportune remark that set in motion a series of tumbles from grace, Sophie had been cut left and right by the young women she'd known her whole life. First came a handful of polite notes with excuses as to why they would not be calling on her. Then came more strongly-worded letters from their mothers rescinding invitations for gatherings Sophie had been looking forward to. Then came nothing at all—no invitations, no calls, and no recognition that Sophie even existed. It was as if she had been written out of the drama of society, all because of the indiscretions of her sisters. And truly, she didn't care that much for the whims of the *ton*. The whole lot of them could sit on a tack.

Except for one—the only one that mattered.

"Come now." Verity approached Sophie as she stepped farther into the shadows of the parlor, in no mood to be lively and gay. "Rebecca's sister Mary might have forbidden Rebecca to know you, but it's not the end of the world."

Sophie sent her sister a doleful look. "It *is* the end of the world. Rebecca is my dearest, bosom friend. I don't know what I shall do without her."

Verity hugged her sister, but when she stepped back, her lips were pursed and she wore a sharp frown. "Lady Mary Burgess is no better than she ought to be," she said. "She's as bad as Lady Charlotte."

It was the worst insult Verity could hurl, for Lady Charlotte Grey was the woman who had started the cascade of dishonor that had led to the Barnes sisters' utter ruin.

At least it felt like utter ruin to Sophie if it meant she and Rebecca could no longer know each other. Verity and Honor both seemed happier than Sophie had known them to be in years. They had rushed into scandalously carnal arrangements with entirely unsuitable men, practically leaping into their beds with abandon at the first opportunity. And while Sophie was devilishly intrigued by the carnal activity that the two couldn't stop talking about, she hadn't met a single man she would care to part her legs and give up her virtue for. None of the men she had ever known were…manly enough. Even if she found such a man, without Rebecca to whisper the tale to, without her to giggle with over the whole thing, all the passion in the world would seem bland.

"I know your heart is wounded, dearest," Verity went on, sliding her arm around Sophie's waist. "But do come and meet some of the guests. I am amazed how exciting some of their lives have been. Being thrown over by the respectable part of society is the best thing that could have happened to me. I have found so many kindred spirits among the dregs of society, and I'm certain you will too."

Tears stung at Sophie's eyes. She was certain Verity meant well, certain she meant to be encouraging. But not even the most fascinating new people could be of comfort when one was still mourning the loss of old friends.

"I think I will continue to observe for a while," she said, slipping away from Verity as subtly as she could. "When I am ready, I will join in."

"Very well, dear." Verity squeezed Sophie's hand, then moved away to seek out her new husband.

Sophie heaved a sigh and moved away from her spot by the doorway. Perhaps if she were seen to be moving about the room no one would bother her. There was much to see—from the way the front of the courtesan, Miss DeRochelle's bodice had slipped so low that her nipples actually sat on top of the neckline instead of being concealed under it, to the sizeable bulge in Lord Matthews' breeches—in the breeches of half the men there, in fact—to the delicious spread of tarts and sweets that decorated a table at one end of the room. There was much to hear as well. Laughter rang freely, as did gossip.

"It's true," Mrs. Clawton, mistress to Lord Tolliver, one of the friends that had cut Sophie and her sisters, was in the middle of saying to two other ladies—Mrs. Glover, the wife of a shop owner from Oxford Street and Mrs. Proctor, the wife of Sebastian's solicitor. "Gosford proposed on Friday, and Lady Charlotte accepted."

"The poor woman," Mrs. Glover said, her eyes wide. "Does she not know how deeply in debt Gosford is?"

"I doubt it," Mrs. Clawton went on. "But I have no sympathy for the woman. She is a bully and a cat, and she deserves what she gets."

Sophie wouldn't disagree with that, but neither was she in the mood to be reminded of Lady Charlotte. Marriage to the odious Lord Gosford would secure the cat's place in good society—a place Sophie was loath to admit she coveted.

"The pirates have been cutting into profits deeply," Captain Templeton, another friend of Lord Landsbury's and Sebastian's, was in the middle of telling a circle of tradesmen and minor noblemen. "I know of two friends who had their ships and cargos stolen right out from under them, in spite of the precautions they'd taken."

"I keep reading about these pirates in the newspaper," Lord Hastings said with a concerned frown. "There have been too many in recent months."

"Too many indeed," Mr. Walters—who owned a cloth mill—agreed with passion. "It is almost as though someone is passing information to the French, alerting them of shipping schedules and routes."

"A spy?" Lord Hastings suggested.

"It would have to be," Mr. Tottenham—a tradesman, like Sebastian, said, scowling. "A spy who has access to shipping records and the ability to pass that information off to the French."

"That could be any number of people, unfortunately," Captain Templeton said. "Anyone with connections to the docks, merchants' associations, even solicitors working with trade contracts."

"Indeed," Lord Hastings agreed.

Sophie moved on, not because she wasn't interested in the possibility of pirates, but because Lord Hastings had spotted her and was raking her with an assessing look, as though she were ripe for the plucking along with the other fallen women in the room. Lord Hastings wasn't bad. He was attractive enough, though he was almost old enough to be her father, and if Lord Landsbury was comfortable having the man in his home, then he was certainly the sort who could be trusted. But Sophie wasn't half as comfortable being the object of sexual interest as her sisters were. Or rather, the flutters that such attention stirred in her were beyond what she was ready to embrace. Besides, if she were of a mind to abandon her virtue, she would want to be the one to pick out the gentleman, not the other way around.

Her circuit of the room took her to the refreshment table. At last, there was something she could turn her attention to. The sweets on offer were like nothing Sophie had ever seen. There were tiny cakes decorated with miniature roses and domed puddings that oozed chocolatey goodness. But there were also confections that would have made her laugh and blush if she'd been in a more jovial mood, including bonbons shaped and colored like breasts, complete with pert, pink nipples, and éclairs detailed to appear exactly like the male genitalia.

"These look divine." One of the courtesans—who went by the single name Evangeline—approached the table and took one of the éclairs. She bit into the tip, then let out a gasp of surprise as thick cream squirted out one side and, presumably, into her mouth. She laughed, and when she had swallowed, she said, "Just like the real thing. Jonathan, you are a genius."

"My deepest thanks, Evangeline."

Sophie caught her breath and turned to find the most extraordinarily handsome and exotic-looking man she'd ever laid eyes on approaching the table. He was tall, with broad shoulders and a narrow waist. He was obviously wealthy, judging by the superior cut of his clothing and the diamond pin in his cravat. But his skin was too bronzed to be merely tanned, and his close-cut hair was textured instead of smooth. Sophie narrowed her eyes to study him. His features were patrician, and yet...not. Her mind told her he was African, and yet the moniker didn't seem to fit what she was seeing. It was as if he existed in a suspended state—not one thing or the other. Like her. He was...he was *manly*. Her heart was instantly drawn to him.

It wasn't until he darted a sideways look in her direction and an impish grin pulled at his tempting lips that Sophie realized she'd been caught staring.

"Oh, I'm so sorry," she said, heat spilling into her face. She took a step back, blinking rapidly in embarrassment and looking for a way to escape. "I shouldn't stare."

"I don't mind," the man said, turning to face her fully. "As long as you don't mind if I stare right back."

His eyes met hers with a heated intensity, and Sophie couldn't look away. Then his gaze dropped to her lips, her neck, her breasts, and lower. It wasn't the usual sort of look a man might give her, not even the lascivious sort. He took her in as an artist might before laying his hands on clay in an attempt to shape it to what was seen. It was as though his hands studied her as well as his eyes. The intensity of his gaze left her shivering, with heat pooling low in her belly.

"Jonathan Foster." He bowed deeply to her. "Sugar merchant and confectioner."

Sophie's eyes went wide. "Did you make these?" she asked, glancing over the treats on the table.

"I did," Jonathan said with a modest bow and a blush that brought the most interesting colors to his cheeks. Not unlike the blush on some of the sugar paste decorating the cakes. She blinked and took a closer look at the cakes. The decorations weren't roses at all. They were petals of an entirely more intimate, feminine kind.

"Good heavens, I've just realized what those ones are," she said with a fluttery laugh, feeling hotter than she thought possible.

"These?" Jonathan reached for one of the cakes in question. "They're a personal favorite of mine."

He raised the cake to his lips, but instead of biting straight into it, he licked at the sugar paste in what she felt was a demonstration of his skill in carnal areas. His gaze remained fixed on Sophie. She had the uncanny sensation of responding to the way he tasted his creation as if it were her petals he was savoring, not the sugar paste ones. Not only that, her nipples tightened, and her breasts felt far heavier and warmer than they should. All of her felt warm.

At last, he popped the tiny cake into his mouth with a chuckle. As soon as he'd chewed and swallowed he said, "Forgive me, Miss Barnes. I shouldn't tease you that way without your permission."

Sophie pressed a hand to her racing heart. "You know who I am?"

"Of course," he answered with a nod of his head. "You are the most beautiful woman in the room."

His words were clearly designed to flatter and flirt, but dammit, Sophie's knees went wobbly all the same. No man had ever flirted with her in such a way before, especially not one as unique as Jonathan Foster.

"Your new brother-in-law also pointed you out to me when I first arrived," Jonathan went on, a mischievous sparkle in his eyes.

"Which one?" Sophie asked, too breathless for her own good.

"Lord Landsbury," Jonathan answered.

"You know Thomas?" It was the sort of question a ninny would ask, but Sophie found herself wanting to converse with Jonathan for as long as possible without having the first clue what she should talk about. Truth be told, she merely wanted him to continue to look at her as though she were a sweet he was about to devour.

"Lord Landsbury's family and my father's family have known each other for generations," he said.

Sophie blinked, the heat within her ebbing a bit. "They have? That seems un—" She bit her tongue as soon as she realized how inappropriate her next words would have been.

Jonathan didn't appear to be offended. In fact, his rakish grin grew. "My father is Lord Foster of Kingston, Jamaica. My mother was formerly his slave, then his mistress. He freed her, then gave her the option of setting up a new life anywhere in the world she desired or staying with him. She chose to stay with him, and—" he spread his arms, "—here I am."

Sophie's mouth dropped open as she studied him. His mixed parentage explained his rare appearance, but his background raised a thousand other questions in her. Questions she wasn't certain were appropriate, but that she wasn't clever enough to stop herself from blurting, such as, "What are you doing in London?"

The answering grin he sent her was both patient and charmed. "In addition to owning a sugar plantation, my father owns a sugar brokerage. I lead the London office."

"Oh?" Sophie wanted to know more, but had no idea how to ask.

Jonathan seemed to sense her interest. "I buy and sell sugar from our plantation and others and arrange trade deals," he said.

"I'm an abolitionist," Sophie blurted before she could think better of it. She winced as soon as the words were out of her mouth. "I mean, the sugar trade is abominable." She winced harder. "No, I mean…I mean…."

"My father is an abolitionist as well," Jonathan interrupted in what might have been an attempt to save her. "As am I. And yes, we are in the thick of an industry that is rife with evils, but we believe that change comes from the inside."

"Yes, of course," Sophie agreed. "Forgive me for prying and for being such a goose about it."

"Not at all." Jonathan's smile grew, and Sophie was certain it was genuine. "Most Londoners blush and look the other way and avoid the topic entirely. I would rather see and be seen for who I am and for the realities that exist."

Something warm and hopeful spilled through Sophie's heart. "I feel the same way," she said in a small voice. It was if all the emotion that had stormed around her since The Disaster coalesced into a moment of understanding.

It was also in that moment that she realized her hand still rested over her heart, or more specifically, over her breast. She moved it away quickly. Jonathan must have thought she'd been standing there through the whole conversation fondling herself.

"That's better," he said, a wicked gleam in his eyes. "You shouldn't hide the beauty God has given you."

Sophie's face went hot. "I wouldn't say He gave me as much as all that."

"I would," Jonathan said, glancing at her form again with frank appreciation. "The body is something to be celebrated, not hidden."

"Perhaps in the Caribbean," Sophie said. "It is simply too cold in London to walk about without clothes." Her pulse jumped at the boldness of her words. Perhaps she did belong with the guests Honor and Sebastian had invited to celebrate their wedding after all. Especially considering the excitement that coursed through her when Jonathan smiled wolfishly at her comment.

She expected him to make some manner of teasingly lewd comment or to proposition her. He surprised her by saying, "Miss Sophie, would you be interested in a job?"

The question was so far from anything Sophie expected that she held her breath and blinked rapidly at him. "A…job? As in employment?" She'd never considered employment, but if her chances for a respectable marriage were gone, it wasn't that much of a stretch for her to seek wages to support herself.

"Yes," Jonathan answered. His smile was so mischievous and alluring that Sophie ached to know what he was thinking. In truth, she merely ached. In certain places in particular.

"I have no skills," she admitted, lowering her head by a few degrees. "My education was never completed, as my father passed away and George no longer wished to pay for our governess."

"I'm sorry to hear that," Jonathan said with a look of genuine sympathy in his eyes. "Education is the key to a successful life. But it is not required for the position I have in mind for you."

In spite of the ignorance Sophie knew she wallowed in,

she smirked at his comment. "My sisters have informed me all about the positions men have for women."

Jonathan laughed, the sound rich and resonant. "We can discuss advancement in this particular position of employment some other time," he said in a way that both piqued Sophie's curiosity about what he wanted her to do and left no doubt in her mind that he would bed her if she showed so much as a hint of interest. She wasn't sure she had enough of her sister's boldness to broach the subject, but thankfully, she didn't have to. "I am hosting an important banquet in two days' time," Jonathan said. "I would like to employ you as decoration."

It seemed there was no end to the ways Jonathan could surprise her. "Decoration?" She shook her head, not understanding.

"Of a unique and scandalous nature," he went on, his grin growing downright devilish. "It is a job that will turn heads and send gossips' tongues wagging."

"That sounds exciting," she said. Indeed, it did. Moreover, it was the first time Sophie had felt excited about something since The Disaster.

"Would you be willing to shock and potentially outrage the cream of high society?" he asked, arching one brow.

Sophie bit her lip, wondering if he knew how the *ton* had treated her and her sisters. She wondered if he could see inside of her and if he knew how desperately a part of her wanted to seek revenge against the likes of Lady Charlotte and Rebecca's sister Mary. She hadn't known that part of her existed, but suddenly, there it was. Society had cast her aside and treated her as though she had ceased to exist, and Jonathan Foster appeared to be offering her the perfect chance to remind them that she was there, she was Sophie Barnes, and she would not be forgotten.

"I would be delighted to scandalize the *ton* in any way I

can," she said, her heart racing. No doubt he intended for her to serve at his banquet and to spill heapings of sticky sugar syrup—or even indelible red wine—on ladies and gentlemen who thought they were better than everyone else.

"I am pleased to hear it," Jonathan said.

He took up her hand and raised it to his lips for a kiss. Sophie remembered the way he had teased the sugar paste decoration on the miniature cake with his lips and tongue, and a zip of erotic energy soared straight to her sex. She found it hard to breathe, and she liked it.

"I will see you in two days," he said, still holding her hand. "Come to the kitchen door of number 12 Park Street at two in the afternoon."

"So early?" she asked.

"We will have quite a bit of preparation for this decoration," he said.

The naughty glint in his eyes was irresistible. Sophie couldn't wait for two days to pass.

"I will be there," she said, warm from head to toe. "And I will be ready for anything."

CHAPTER 2

Sophie kept her plans to work at Jonathan's banquet a secret, even from her sisters. There was something naughty about everything she'd agreed to do for Jonathan—perhaps the fact that she wasn't entirely sure what she had agreed to—and she couldn't bring herself to consult with her sisters about it. In fact, the very idea that she had something wicked of her own waiting around the corner, something that she hadn't fallen into accidentally or had thrust on her because of her sisters' scandalous behavior, was as delectable as the sugary treats Jonathan had provided for Honor and Sebastian's wedding. She had a secret, and she adored it.

Jonathan hadn't given her much in the way of instructions, but she was determined to follow what little he'd told her as closely as possible. She arrived at number 12 Park Street precisely when she was expected and knocked on the kitchen door, her heart beating in her throat with excitement. Almost immediately, the door was opened by a tall, handsome woman with her hair caught up in a cap.

"Miss Sophie Barnes?" she asked.

Sophie nodded. "That is me."

The woman smiled, raked her with a glance from head to toe, and motioned for her to come inside. "Follow me, please."

The woman led her into a massive kitchen teeming with cooks. Sweet, fragrant steam swirled up from half a dozen stoves. Sharp citrus and mellow chocolate scents filled the air. Sophie's mouth watered as the woman led her through the frenzied activity of people stirring pots, pouring chocolate into molds, and chopping mincemeat.

"Mr. Foster didn't tell me what I should wear to his banquet," she chattered to relieve some of her anxiety as they turned a corner and headed down a second hall.

The handsome woman paused and glanced at her in surprise. "He didn't tell you?"

"He only asked if I would be willing to help him perpetrate a scandal on the *ton*," she said, wondering if she should be a bit more circumspect with a servant she knew nothing about.

The woman studied her carefully before heading on. "I don't believe you're prepared for what Mr. Foster has in mind."

"Oh, but I am," Sophie insisted. "My life has taken such a strange turn that I am prepared for anything."

"Anything?" the woman asked, then pushed open a door.

The room she led Sophie into was small and humid. A large, copper tub sat near a cozy fire, its water steaming. Rose petals floated on its surface.

"Undress and bathe," the woman instructed her. "I'll prepare the sugar wax."

Sophie stopped a few steps into the room and stared first at the bath, then at the woman as she moved to a small table next to the hearth. "You want me to undress and bathe?" she asked.

"Yes," the woman said without a pause in her work. "It's what you're here for, after all."

Sophie wanted to ask, "Is it?" but she wasn't brave enough. Or rather, she was too brave to ask the sort of questions that would lead to her losing her nerve, turning tail, and running. She stepped to the side of the room where a rack stood to hold her clothes and began to undress.

"I take it you will be attending my bath?" she asked, not entirely certain how she felt undressing completely in front of a woman she'd only just met. She'd undressed in front of her sisters and mother plenty of times from earliest childhood, and she'd even stripped down to almost nothing with Rebecca and their friends a time or two to swim in the pond near Georgiana Travers's family's country estate, but that was different.

The woman glanced over her shoulder at Sophie. "Of course," she said, then returned to her work of cutting linen strips.

To ask what the woman was doing would have betrayed just how ignorant Sophie was, so she continued undressing until she was completely nude, though her hands shook just a bit. As soon as the last of her things were folded and placed over the rack, she skittered to the tub and stepped inside.

"Ahh!" She sank into the fragrant water with all the appreciation that the luxury of a warm bath brought with it. She'd never managed to soak in a tub with water quite as warm as her current bath, and certainly not one filled with rosewater. It was so good that she closed her eyes and leaned against the side of the tub.

"Take care not to wet your hair," the woman said. She'd moved from cutting strips of linen to mixing something sweet-smelling in a small caldron over the fire. "Mr. Foster would like it dry for the display."

Again, Sophie was tempted to ask what display, but with

each second that ticked by, she was less and less inclined to let on that she didn't have the first idea what was going on.

"Be sure to scrub well," the woman said. "It's better if you are completely clean."

"Yes," Sophie agreed and took the rag hanging over the side of the tub.

She gave her whole body a quick scrub, even parts she was embarrassed to wash with someone else in the room. What if the whole point of the ablution was because Jonathan intended to ravish her? What if he preferred his conquests to be washed and smelling of roses? She had to admit to herself that she wouldn't have minded if he did.

"Out of the tub now," the woman ordered, though not unkindly, just when Sophie had decided a nice, long soak would be in order. "There isn't much time, and as I dare say you've never had your hair removed with wax, we will likely have much work to do."

"Wax?" Sophie stood, water sluicing over her naked body. She raised her hands to her head. "Hair?"

"Not that hair," the woman laughed. "Come."

She gave Sophie a hand out of the tub and helped her to dry with a thick towel. It was unnerving and odd and strangely arousing to have the woman rubbing her dry as though she were a statue that had just been cleaned. It was even more nerve-wracking when the woman pointed for her to lie on a chaise near the table that held the linen strips and cauldron, which she'd removed from the fire.

"Since you've never had this done before," she explained, "I'll start with your legs. That will give you an idea of how much it hurts. When your legs are clean, we'll move to underarms, and finally pubis."

Sophie wanted to stop the woman in her tracks as she turned to the table and stirred whatever was in the pot. She wanted to demand more of an explanation, and possibly to call the whole thing off and run away, naked or not. Instead, she sat there and held her breath while the woman spread a sort of sticky-sweet honey-like mixture on one of her legs. The sensation was warm and bizarre, and ever so slightly titillating. At least until the woman applied a linen strip, then tore it off.

Sophie shouted in shock as all the hair on her leg where the wax had been applied ripped out and came away with the linen. "What in the name of all that is sacred," she started, but forced herself to relax and catch her breath instead.

The woman grinned at her. "Mr. Foster said you might change your mind when you learned what was involved."

"For heaven's sake, what is involved?" Sophie asked, panting.

"I am to remove all of the hair from your body," the woman said, laughing outright. "Mr. Foster needs a clean canvas to work on, and the guests find a hairless body more appealing."

Sophie merely sat there, gaping at the woman for a moment. Her body a canvas? Guests preferred a hairless body? Good Lord. Jonathan had said she would be a decoration. She'd assumed he was speaking metaphorically. But no, apparently her body, her hairless body, would be on display as a decoration.

Scandalous. Certain to cause shock and outrage. Heads would turn and gossips' tongues would wag.

Well.

Something dark and determined welled up within Sophie. If this was what it took to make the *ton* recognize that she still existed in spite of their attempts to erase her from society, then so be it. She would eclipse everything her sisters had done to complete their falls from grace, because she would be doing it in public.

"Go on," she said with a gulp, offering her leg to the woman so that she could continue.

The best Sophie could say about the experience was that the woman was proficient at her task. If she had tried to apply the wax and the strips and yank all her hair out herself, she would have lost her nerve. But the woman knew what she was doing. She worked so quickly that Sophie barely had time to flinch with each new section of hair that was wrenched violently from her.

It was far more difficult to swallow her yelps of pain when the woman removed the hair from her underarms. But Sophie nearly lost her nerve when the woman instructed her to spread her legs so that she could remove every bit of hair from her unmentionable regions. She'd accepted that she might end up with her legs parted if she agreed to Jonathan's scheme, but never could she have foreseen a woman who was taller and more muscular than her brother staring intently at her nether regions. She first took a small pair of scissors to Sophie's curls to remove the bulk of the hair, then mercilessly smeared hot, sweet wax across the region, then ripped her hair from her skin. In short, it was agony.

"All done," the woman said at last with a comforting smile. She retrieved a second bowl from the table and began to dab a small, soft sponge soaked in some sort of soothing unction on the red and raw skin between Sophie's legs. "You did exceptionally well for your first time. Most girls scream and cry for hours afterward. This mixture will soothe and cool your skin and prevent redness and bumps."

Sophie wasn't about to tell the woman she was on the verge of tears. Whatever concoction she was bathing her wounded nethers in did feel good, though. It smelled faintly of cucumber and something else herby. And after a few more minutes, the pain subsided altogether, leaving Sophie with a tingling sensation that was not unpleasant. Of course, that could have been due to the way the wax woman continued to brush the sponge over her tender flesh. It made her suddenly aware that she lay before the woman completely nude and exposed to view.

"No wonder Mr. Foster singled you out," the woman said at last with a sigh, standing to straighten the table and her tools. "Your body is delicious."

Sophie bit her lip and glanced down at herself. She hadn't been that bare since she was a girl. She'd never been half as sensitive in those areas either. And she had a feeling she'd only just begun her adventure for the day.

"Here's a robe you can wear," the wax woman said, returning to a more businesslike demeanor. "I'll take you up to the banquet room."

Sophie donned the robe and followed the woman out of the room and through the winding corridors to the main part of the house. Part of her whispered that she should be disturbed by what had just happened and alarmed for what was to come, but it was as if the pain had pushed her so far out of what was normal that her mind was soft and ready to accept every sort of strangeness that came her way.

"Ah, Miss Barnes. You are right on time," Jonathan greeted her as the wax woman brought her into a magnificent ballroom that was decorated from the floor to the rafters. "Thank you, Glenda," Jonathan nodded to the wax woman.

"Sir." Glenda curtsied, sent Sophie the sort of saucy, flirty look she would have expected to receive from a man, then turned and headed back the way they'd come.

"Don't mind Glenda," Jonathan said, offering her a hand. "She flirts with everyone."

"I see." Sophie decided not to mention the special attention Glenda had given after denuding her.

She took Jonathan's hand, and he led her across the room

to a long, wide banquet table that was already half covered with flowers and trays of confections. The entire perimeter of the room was stacked high with the most gorgeous cakes and tarts, jellies and candies that Sophie had ever seen. It was as if each table were its own scene in a play that was about to unfold, or like the stages of the cross that she'd been told Catholics walked between while at their prayers.

"Everything is so beautiful," she said, trying to take it all in at once. "Did you make all of this?"

"Not all of it," Jonathan laughed. "I designed each centerpiece and made the key elements, but my assistants carried out most of the supporting work."

"It's brilliant," she said. Her admiring gaze returned to him. He wore only a simple shirt and waistcoat with an apron tied over that, but the informality of his dress filled Sophie with a sense of intimacy and adventure. They were not in the polite drawing rooms of society anymore.

As soon as they reached what was clearly the table that would hold the showpiece of the banquet, Jonathan stopped and let go of her hand. "Your robe, Miss Barnes."

"You can call me Sophie," she said. A moment later, she realized what he was asking. A squeak escaped from her before she could stop it. "You want me to take off my robe right now? With everyone in the room?"

One of Jonathan's assistants who was close enough to hear the exchange as he added icing to a table of chocolate treats laughed and made a show of watching her. Jonathan didn't exactly seem angered by the bold gesture, but he shook his head at the man.

"Everybody out," he called, turning to the handful of assistants who rushed around the room working on the sweets.

A few people made sounds of disappointment, and one young man in particular looked as though Jonathan was ordering him away from his firstborn child, but they all left within a minute. That left Sophie and Jonathan alone, still standing face-to-face.

Jonathan held out a hand. "Your robe," he repeated.

Sophie caught her breath. She could do this. It wasn't that she didn't want to bare her hairless body to Jonathan. In fact, the trouble was that she wanted to show him a little too eagerly. The arousal she felt at the very idea was more than she was prepared for. But she'd vowed to herself that she would go through with everything, so she pulled at the sash holding her robe closed to undo it, then shrugged out of the thin garment and handed it over to Jonathan.

Every inch of her skin tingled as he looked at her. His gaze swept her body with a frank, male appreciation that left Sophie's breath coming in shallow gasps. She was only feet away from him, more naked than naked, without even hair to hide herself from him. And dear heavens above, he looked as though he wanted to slide his hands over every part of her that had been treated to such torture earlier. Sophie couldn't help but think that his touch between her legs would be a thousand times more soothing than Glenda's cucumber ministrations.

"Up on the table," Jonathan said at last in a gruff voice.

Sophie blinked, then noticed a small step-ladder placed in front of the table as stairs. Other things became apparent to her as well. A white, silk pad was laid out on the table like a palate. Several small cushions were arranged across it. The table itself held a variety of bowls and containers of bonbons, marzipan, sugar paste, and sugars in several colors.

"You want me on the table?" she asked, embarrassed by the squeak in her voice.

"Lying down," Jonathan confirmed, taking her hand and leading her to the step-ladder. "We'll work out the most comfortable position for you. You may have to hold it for several hours."

Sophie was grateful to Glenda for prompting her to use the chamber pot before taking her to the banquet hall. She shook slightly as she climbed the ladder to the tabletop. It was wildly unusual to walk on a table and even wilder to recline across a bed of silk and cushions. But the strangest feeling of all came when Jonathan's eyes took on a craftsman's focus instead of the lust of a man in his prime.

"Rest your head back this way," he said, grasping her head gently and maneuvering it to one of the cushions. He pulled the pins out of her style and raked through her loose hair with his fingers, fanning it around her like a halo. "We'll brush it once more before the guests arrive. As for the rest of your body...."

He let his words fade into the concentration of an artist sculpting. Sophie's heart raced as he arranged her arms gently above her head, giving her no way whatsoever to cover her chest. He placed a cushion under her back, adjusted her hips, and placed her legs slightly parted, one knee bent.

"You're a dream to work with, Sophie," he purred once he had her how he wanted her. "Your body is so lithe and nimble, and you move so easily as I want you to."

His words carried a heat to them that suggested far more than the living sculpture he had created with her. Her sex ached and her breasts felt full. A little too much so.

"My legs," she said, continuing to hold perfectly still as he moved to the side to go through his bowls of sugar and tools.

"What about them?" he asked as he returned with a large container of powdered sugar and a sort of sieve.

Sophie cleared her throat. "The way you've arranged them, anyone who stands at that end of the table will be able to look right at my...." She pressed her lips shut. Whatever word she used to describe her sex would only sound silly.

Jonathan leaned closer to her ear, so close that his breath brushed her cheek, making her nipples hard. "That is exactly the point, my beauty."

Sophie was speechless as he stepped back, furrowed his brow into a frown, and proceeded to dust her body with powdered sugar. She caught her breath, even though the sugar was too light to be felt. It didn't matter. Every inch of her skin came alive with excitement. When Jonathan finished with his base coat of sugar, he went to work with everything else he had. He painted trailing vines of flowers with thin icing on her arms and legs. He shaded her torso with colored sugar in peach and pink and yellow. He used marzipan and sugar paste to transform her breasts into luscious mounds of confectionary and arranged crystalized sugar gems in the hollow of her neck like a necklace. He painted her lips with chocolate and covered them with colorful nonpareils. And through the whole thing, Sophie somehow managed to stay utterly still.

At least, her body remained still. Her mind was swimming in heady, carnal madness as he reformed her into a delicacy. Every part of her wanted to cry out for him to ravage her in all the ways her sisters had talked about their husbands making love to them. She felt so much like she was on fire that she didn't know how the sweets decorating her skin didn't melt.

And then he shifted to decorate her pubis.

"I'm glad to see you're enjoying your employment, my sweet," Jonathan said in a deep, sensual, teasing voice as he took a damp rag to cleanse her sex.

Sophie sucked in a breath as he rubbed the cloth over flesh that was inflamed to the point of sending her over the edge. She knew she needed to remain still, but her breathing became shallow and ragged as he took his time. She even stooped to letting out a sound of desperation, practically begging him to bring her release.

"Not yet, my beauty," he said, laughter in his voice as he moved his hand away, dabbed the area he'd washed dry, then sprinkled powdered sugar over her. "I want you seething with need as my guests feast on the sight of you," he continued in a whisper that was like torture. "I want them to look at you, suspended in pleasure without release, and to desire you as much as I do."

It was the wrong time for him to mention his desire for her. Or perhaps the right time. The agony of desire without release pounded harder within her. She would have done anything to set free the coil of pleasure winding tighter and tighter inside of her. She'd never known such hopeless, helpless longing was possible. And now she knew he wanted her.

"That's it," he said, making things so much worse as he painted icing across her exposed sex and arranged sugar paste decorations. "Feed that desire within you. Let it smolder. Let it burn. If you radiate sex for my guests, I will reward you beyond your wildest dreams at the end of the night."

Instantly, images of him stripping off his clothes, climbing on the table with her, and impaling her with what she was certain was a mighty organ, assailed her. But she had to stay still. She couldn't mar all of his intricate work. She had to do what she'd come there for. She had to make him proud.

"There," he said, stepping back at last and easing the desire that throbbed through her. "I think we're just about ready. "One more thing."

She lay where she was, unable to move her neck so that she could follow where he went. Moments later, he returned with a sumptuous piece of white silk, exactly like what she lay on. He shook the silk out, then lay it over the top half of her face, covering everything above her lips and all the way up to the top of her forehead.

"Why?" she asked. The single syllable was all she was capable of without cracking the chocolate on her lips.

"I want my guests feasting on your body, my sweet," he explained. "I don't want them knowing your identity. For your sake as well as mine." A wave of disappointment swept through Sophie that calmed the lust that had been blazing within her. "I want people to talk about the delectable beauty on my table, not to gossip about Miss Sophie Barnes debasing herself for the son of a slave."

He had a point. One she couldn't very well argue with, either physically or mentally. But just because the high and mighty of the *ton* wouldn't know Sophie Barnes was on display, wearing nothing but sugar, didn't mean the effect and the scandal wouldn't be as potent.

A knock sounded at the far end of the room and a door opened. The rush of dozens of voices talking flowed in.

"Sir, your guests are growing impatient," someone said.

"Let them in, Harmon," Jonathan gave the order. "We're ready now."

CHAPTER 3

*P*anic coursed through Sophie as the sound of dozens of people rushed into the room. At no point had she stopped to consider how many people would be attending Jonathan's banquet. She'd assumed a handful at most, but it sounded as though an entire ball's worth of ladies and gentlemen marched into the room, chattering, exclaiming, and marveling at everything they saw.

"Don't worry," Jonathan said. Sophie heard him slide the step-ladder she'd used to climb onto her perch under the table. "I will be standing nearby, as will Freddy." She assumed he referred to one of his assistants. "If anyone makes a move to touch you, they will be stopped."

Sophie nodded slightly, but fear and the absolute need to stay perfectly still in case the decorations covering her cracked kept her mostly immobile.

She felt Jonathan move away, and as he stepped aside, a ripple of gasps followed. With her eyes covered she couldn't see to be certain, but she had a good idea that she'd been noticed.

"Good Lord! Look at that," a male voice said, rushing toward her.

Sophie felt people approach. Her heart thumped against her ribs so hard that she was certain it was visible to everyone staring at her naked body. Then again, as the whispered comments reached her ears, she was well aware it wasn't her heartbeat people were looking at.

"Those tits look delicious," a man said in a ribald tone.

"I'd take a bite out of one of them any day," his friend replied with a chuckle.

"You don't bite them," a third man said. "You suckle and savor them."

All three men laughed. The sound and their comments were rude, but they had the paradoxical effect of stoking the fire of need that Jonathan had lit in Sophie.

The sensual feeling grew as more people wandered by to gaze at her.

"It's obscene," a woman gasped. Sophie felt a brush of air, as though she were fanning herself. "Everything is on display. *Everything.*"

"It most certainly is," a man said in a much more appreciative voice. Sophie felt the woman move on before the man murmured to someone, "That cunny looks good enough to eat."

A woman laughed in low, teasing tones. "Would you like to watch me gobble up that tart?"

Sophie's eyebrows shot up under the silk that concealed her face.

The man growled lustily. "We'd better move on before I unman myself at the thought."

The woman laughed, and the two walked away. They were quickly replaced by others, though. Within minutes, Sophie understood exactly what it meant to be the showpiece of the banquet.

"Is she real?" a man asked from only feet away. "I don't think she's real."

"Of course she's real," a woman said. "Watch carefully and you can see her breathing."

Sophie instantly held her breath.

"She's not moving at all. I don't think she is real," the man said.

"Please don't touch, my lord," Jonathan's firm voice said just as Sophie felt a hand near her stomach. "She is real."

"Good heavens," the man said. "She's naked."

"You're just seeing that now?" the woman with him asked.

"I thought she was sugar before," the man went on. "But this is…this is extraordinary."

More people moved past. Sophie began to relax into her role. She felt their eyes on her, felt the lust they were experiencing. More than half of the comments whispered beside her were appreciative and sultry, though a few people were desperately offended. Sophie paid them no mind. Her sincerest hope was that Jonathan would gain business from her display.

"George. George, come stand here," a man said from somewhere near her feet.

A moment of desperate panic hit Sophie as she imagined her brother George seeing her as she was.

"Good Lord, you can see every bit of her cunt," the man, presumably George, said.

Sophie breathed an inward sigh of relief. It wasn't her brother. Plenty of men were named George.

"Is that sugar syrup or is she wet?" George whispered to his friend.

"Dear God, I think she's wet," the friend said. "The little tart is loving every second of this."

"Ha! Tart," George snorted, then said, "Dammie, man, get

your hand away from your breeches. The room is full of people."

"There must be a retiring room around here somewhere," George's friend said in an urgent voice before rushing off.

Sophie wanted to laugh, but she kept perfectly still. Who would have thought that disgraced, invisible Sophie Barnes could inspire men to abuse themselves at a public event? It didn't even matter that they didn't know who she was.

"*Ça y est. C'est parfait*," a man spoke by Sophie's side. She felt him lean in close.

"Please don't touch, my lord," Jonathan said for what felt like the hundredth time in the evening.

"I wasn't touching," the man snapped in perfect English, without an accent. The voice was familiar, but Sophie couldn't place it.

"How do you mean it's perfect," a woman's voice asked in the softest of whispers. Sophie recognized that voice as well, but without being able to see, she had no idea who was speaking.

"*En français. C'est plus sûr de cette façon*," the man went on. "*In French. It's safer that way.*"

"*Safer?*" the woman responded in French. "*Half the people in the room speak French.*"

"*I doubt he does*," the man said, no doubt referring to Jonathan. "*Or this whore.*"

Sophie's gut clenched, but there was nothing she could do but lie as she was and listen. She'd been tutored in French extensively before George dismissed her governess, and she prided herself on speaking it like a native. She and Rebecca and their friends had spent many an afternoon conversing solely in French.

Her indignant thoughts were cut short as the man went on with, "*The confections. Don't you see? They are perfect for our needs.*"

"*I do not see how*," the woman said.

"*The authorities have grown suspicious*," the man continued. "*They have nearly traced the information we've sent to Langlais on several occasions.*"

"*I never did trust that man*," the woman said. "*I don't care if he works for the French government or not, the man is a blood-thirsty pirate.*"

Sophie nearly gasped at the comment. Her heart raced, and it was harder than ever to remain still.

"Shove on there," someone commented behind the man and woman. "We're waiting to get a look at the sugar tits."

"Wait your turn," the man growled. Sophie felt him turn back to the table before he said to the woman in French, "*Look at all these sweets and cakes and tarts. They're precisely the sort of things the French adore. It would be child's play to order a shipment to be sent to Paris.*"

"*To what end?*" the woman asked.

"*We write out the names and itineraries of the merchant vessels on small slips of paper and insert them in cakes. My man has secured information regarding a dozen or more East India ships and the routes they are planning. Langlais will pay generously for information like that.*"

"*It would make him richer than a sultan*," the woman agreed. "*Us as well. And all we'd have to do is plant our messages in cakes.*"

"*If worst came to worst*," the man went on, "*we could blame the mulatto. No one would suspect us when we could point to him.*"

"*Brilliant*," the woman said. "*I always knew you were clever.*"

"Move on," the man standing behind the pair said, even less patient than before.

"All right, all right," the man snapped. "We've had enough of a look at this cheap tart anyhow."

The pair moved on, but part of Sophie wished they hadn't. She longed to pull the silk from her eyes to get a good look at who they were. They were spies, perhaps the very

THE DELECTABLE TART

spies who had been feeding information to the French pirates everyone had been talking about at Honor and Sebastian's wedding party. Sophie was certain of it, and yet, she couldn't do a thing to stop them.

JONATHAN STOOD AT THE HEAD OF THE TABLE WHERE SOPHIE lay, wrestling with emotions and impulses that were millimeters from getting away from him. His banquet showed every sign of being a tremendous success. Nearly two hundred invitations had been sent out, promising sweets and surprises as a showcase for his confectionary talent. It was encouraging to see that at least two-thirds of the people he'd invited had arrived. His assistants had informed him that several people who didn't have invitations had come as well, but as long as they were potential customers, Jonathan was more than happy to let them in.

The trouble was, as much as the assembly of wealth and privilege gaped and exclaimed in awe, as much as they moaned with pleasure at the sample cakes his assistants were handing out, alarmingly few of them had asked him for menus and price lists. He needed the banquet to be more than a spectacle. If he ever hoped to be more than his father's mouthpiece in London, he needed to establish himself for the art that fueled his purpose for being alive.

He steadied his faltering nerves by studying Sophie. A smile instantly replaced the tight line that had become of his mouth. He was impressed. Beyond impressed. He'd taken a huge chance by inviting virginal Miss Sophie Barnes to become the centerpiece of his banquet. His first impression of her at Sebastian's wedding celebration was that she was sweet, naïve, a little sad, and fragile. Sebastian and Thomas had told him all about her unfortunate fall from grace, but he'd never dreamed that, even under those circumstances, she would be willing to bare everything for him. All he'd seen at the party was her glorious shape and sensual lips.

Her body was magnificent. He couldn't have asked for a finer canvas. Her stomach was flat and her waist thin. Her breasts were full and inviting with a natural pertness that made him as randy as the guests that gawped at her with obvious lust. Her thighs had just the right amount of flesh to make them shapely. And when she'd first disrobed to reveal her silky-smooth sex, he'd been tempted to abandon the banquet entirely so that he could touch her and taste her and spend the rest of the evening burying his cock deep in that smoothness. It had been all he could do not to come in his breeches when he'd discovered how wet she was while decorating her.

"Mr. Foster, your work is divine." An approaching duke startled Jonathan out of his increasingly heated thoughts, and he was grateful for it.

"Thank you, your grace," he said with a respectful bow.

The duke sidled closer to him and murmured, "Is the girl for sale? You know, for an after-banquet feast." He flickered on eyebrow lasciviously.

"I'm afraid she is not, your grace," Jonathan told the man with a straight face. "But the rest of the confections are, as are my services to create more for any special occasion you may have."

The duke sighed in disappointment. "'Tis a pity," he said, then slipped into a mischievous look. "Not even for a guinea?"

"I'm sorry, your grace," Jonathan said.

The duke slid closer still, lowering his voice to a low purr. "Ten pounds. I'll give you ten pounds to let me fuck the sugar right off her at the close of the banquet."

A possessive rush filled Jonathan. If anyone was going to fuck Sophie at the end of the banquet it was going to be him.

THE DELECTABLE TART

If anyone was going to have their way with her at all, even beyond the banquet, it would be him. It was a shock to feel so strongly, but he wanted Sophie all for himself.

He thought quickly, sending the duke a conspiratorial look. "Your grace, I did not want to reveal this. In fact, I made a solemn promise not to say a thing on pain of death, but it is highly possible that the woman in question is a member of the royal family."

The duke stepped back, his eyes wide. "No," he gasped, then laughed and glanced to Sophie. Clearly, he believed Jonathan's lie. "That would be just like them," he chuckled. He slapped Jonathan on the back. "What a coup, what a coup. Old George would go madder than he already is to hear of this."

The duke walked away, laughing. Jonathan smiled until he was certain the man was no longer paying attention to him, then his face dropped. The bugger hadn't asked about cakes or even hinted that he would like to hire him. His career might have been set if a man of the duke's importance asked him to provide sweets for just one event, but no. All they wanted was Sophie.

"Mr. Foster, it is ten o'clock," Freddy informed him.

Jonathan nodded. "Clear the banquet hall," he said. "Make certain that each guest leaves with a leaflet advertising our services and with cakes to take home."

Giving away sugar was a mind-boggling expense, but if it brought in business, it would be worth it.

"Ladies and gentlemen, if you could please make your way toward the exit," Freddy announced near the door.

Slowly, the crowd of high and mighty left the tables—most of which had been thoroughly picked over and devoured—and wandered out of the room. A few people lingered and loitered, and Jonathan spotted at least one man shoving as many tarts and bonbons as he could into a poorly-concealed sack. Jonathan shook his head, but it would have been too much of a scene to confront the man where he was. He glanced across the room to Freddy, making his assistant aware of the sweet thief and trusting him to take necessary precautions. He himself had other things to do.

"We'll clean up in the morning," he announced to his staff, some of whom had already begun to gather up the few, scattered leftovers and remove non-edible decorations from tables. "For now, you can all go. You've done well tonight."

"Thank you, sir," a few of them called before finishing a few tidying chores and heading out of the room.

Jonathan suspected they knew full well why he wanted them to leave the room. He turned toward Sophie with a hungry grin. Every last ounce of tension and uncertainty he'd had to endure was worth it with such a treat waiting for him. He walked to the center of the table and lifted the band of silk from her face.

Sophie's eyes fluttered open, but still she didn't move.

"You did magnificently," he told her, pride pulsing through him along with the lust he'd barely kept in check all night. "I'm amazed that you could hold still for so long."

She moved her mouth to speak, but the chocolate he'd painted on her lips earlier had fused her lips together. It cracked and she made a noise, but words were beyond her. For the moment.

"Let me help you with that, my sweet," he said.

The treats that had been on offer in front of Sophie had all been taken away, so all Jonathan had to do was sweep aside a few remaining flowers and bunches of silk before sitting on the side of the table. From there, he braced one arm on the other side of Sophie, then bent over her to nibble and kiss the chocolate away from her mouth.

It was the most delicious treat he had ever tasted. The chocolate melted in his mouth, but it was the saltier taste of her lips that captivated him. He licked her chin and drew his tongue across the remnants of sweet surrounding her mouth. Sophie moved then, her body straining toward him in a slow, subtle gyration.

As soon as her lips were freed, she took a breath and parted them. Jonathan took advantage of the movement to slide his tongue into her mouth to play with hers. He half expected her to complain and push him away, breaking her sultry pose at last. Instead, she moaned deep in her throat and imitated his tongue's teasing, kissing him in return.

"You are my sweet," he whispered, kissing and licking the painted sugar flowers from her neck. "I've stood by all evening watching men lust after you, knowing that I would be the one to taste you at last."

"Jonathan." She sighed his name, sending blood straight to his cock. "I—"

"Tell me if you want me to stop," he murmured, nuzzling her neck and brushing the hard candy jewels he'd adorned her collar with so that he could lick away more of the powdered sugar.

"No, I—ohh." She sighed as he kissed his way down the top of her breast before closing his mouth around her candy-coated nipple.

The combination of salt and sweet was deliciously maddening. It seemed a shame to waste such careful decoration by stroking a hand across her belly and closing it around her other breast, but he couldn't help himself. He wanted to give her pleasure as much as he wanted to feast on her and feed the fire within him. Every one of the guests who had commented on the magnificence of her breasts throughout the night was absolutely right. They were a handful, large and soft with wide areolas and nipples that were already pert but hardened into points as he suckled and teased her. He stroked one with his tongue until Sophie made a desperate, panting sound of pleasure.

"You like this, my sweet," he said, his voice ragged with need. He wouldn't ask if she wanted him, wanted what he was doing. He could feel that she did. He'd seen it from the moment she removed her robe. She wanted desperately to be debauched, to be wanton.

He was well aware that he couldn't hold out all night, and with a burst of energy, he mounted the table full, spreading her legs wide and positioning himself between them. Pulse pounding, sweating under his fine clothes, he dipped down to lick the sugar off of her stomach, following the trailing vines he'd painted that led down to her sex.

He was lost in the taste of her and the heat of desire that when she gasped the word, "Spies," it threw him off completely.

He paused with his mouth only inches from his goal. "Spies?"

"They were here," she panted. "I just had to say before… before…." Her chest rose and fell in time with her shallow, gasping breaths. "I can feel your breath against my sex," she said, almost crying.

Jonathan grinned. "Can you?" He tilted his head down and blew gently against the sugared folds of her heat.

She made a desperate sound, but continued to be miraculously still. Her arms were still positioned above her head, where he'd put them. Jonathan was overcome by the sensation that she had submitted completely to him in spite of there being no external bonds. Her body was where he had put it, and in spite of the passionate torment pinching her face and the desperation in her panting breaths, she was at his mercy. He hadn't asked. They hadn't discussed it in advance. She had naturally put herself in his power.

"Does it feel good?" he asked, moving her legs farther apart and inching lower. "That ache you feel?"

"Yes," she sighed heavily. "So good."

He bent toward her cunny and picked away the tiny sugar roses he'd decorated her skin with. She trembled ever so slightly and tilted her head back, but in spite of the tension he could feel radiating from her, she didn't move her hips from where he'd put them.

"You want to come, don't you," he said, feeling like a king.

"Yes," she mewled, her desperation palpable.

He licked the sugar gently from her bare mons and she held her breath, the barest squeal indicating how much pleasure she felt.

"This is driving you mad, isn't it?" he asked, blowing on her dampened skin.

She made a needy sound in reply, evidently beyond words. Her face was contorted and her eyes squeezed closed.

He dipped down to her again, sliding his tongue across her wet slit. The sweetness he tasted was all her own. She caught her breath and let out a passionate, pleading sound.

"What would you do, my sweet, if I kept you suspended like this all night?" he asked, sorely tempted by the idea. "What if I held you in the fire of desire without letting you have release."

"I would go mad," she squeaked.

It was the most honest thing anyone had ever said to Jonathan. She would go mad with lust, and he would too, if he wasn't careful. Sophie's capacity to feel so intimately without letting herself release was devastatingly erotic. He wondered if she even realized that at any time she could move, touch herself, demand he finish her, or any number of things to find relief. Instead, she lay as she did, clearly aflame with need, waiting.

"I like you this way," he growled, sliding his hands up her

inner thighs and destroying the careful decorations he'd painted. "I like you hungry and needy and ready. You realize a duke offered me ten pounds to fuck you this evening. Should I call him back? I can see how badly you want it."

"No," she panted, unable to keep completely still anymore. "You. I want you. Only you."

Her answer touched him. She wanted him over a tidy sum and a lover of such high status that it boggled the mind. He couldn't refuse her any longer. He drew his tongue over the hot, damp flesh of her sex again, but instead of teasing her, this time he delved deep. He buried himself in her warmth, finding her clitoris and stroking it with his tongue until she burst.

She cried out as the orgasm hit her, and for a change, he had to hold her thighs firmly to keep her from bucking off the table and writhing with release. Her pussy clenched hard, on and on for an impossible length of time. He wanted to loosen his breeches and bury his cock deep inside her wetness so that she could milk him into release that was already mere inches away. He couldn't hold out, but he knew he had her at a cruel disadvantage, and he wasn't the kind of heartless rake to take a woman when she was too overcome to choose him.

Instead, he fumbled with the fall of his breeches until he was able to take his cock out. He balanced on one hand between her legs and stroked himself mercilessly. A raw cry of passion ripped from him as his seed spilled on the silk between her legs. He would have given anything for it to spill inside of Sophie, but if the way she moved and writhed as her orgasm left her warm and weak, there would be time for that later.

He let go of himself but didn't bother to tuck his mollified cock away as he repositioned himself above her. He planted

THE DELECTABLE TART

his hands on either side of her still stretched arms and brought his face to within inches of hers.

"If you want me fully," he said, his chest rising and falling rapidly as he caught his breath, "if you want me to fuck you so thoroughly that you'll be spoiled for any other man for the rest of your life, come to my flat in Soho in two days."

Sophie seemed to regain a fraction of sense. "You don't live here?"

"This is my father's house," Jonathan said. "I want you at my house."

She stared at him in surprise, but her eyes also held satiety and renewed desire. She still wanted him, perhaps more after everything he'd made her feel. It was enough to fan the flames of his passion for her anew. And yet, he couldn't help but feel as though there were more than simple lust to his infatuation with Sophie Barnes. He'd never met anyone like her, and he would have sacrificed nearly anything to make her his.

CHAPTER 4

"You've been unusually quiet today," Verity commented to Sophie across the table two days later as they enjoyed an early supper. Verity and Thomas were going to the theater that night, and Sophie could hardly form a thought because she'd agreed to go to Jonathan's house for a night of passion.

Passion that she'd experienced the first delicious taste of at the end of the banquet.

Jonathan had taken her by surprise when he climbed onto the table with her and set her blood on fire with his mouth. She'd wanted to tell him what she'd overheard, all about the spies, but as soon as he kissed the chocolate away from her lips, every thought had left her head. Jonathan had brought the low-level ache she'd felt all evening as strangers looked at her to a roaring blaze. His lips and tongue and teeth were a revelation.

"Sophie?"

Every new inch of her skin that he licked and tasted had awakened something within her. The way he'd teased her breasts and suckled her was scandalous beyond measure, but had also made her weak with wanting. It had felt so magical to submit herself fully to every dangerous thing he did to her that she'd been unable to move.

"Sophie, dear?"

Even when he'd done such supremely wicked things to her sex with his mouth. It didn't matter how openly Verity and Honor had discussed their husbands doing exactly those things, feeling it for herself had been heavenly. And hellish, in an odd way. Jonathan had known just how to bring her to the point of bursting and then to deny her that release. Thinking back to the encounter, he had only held her suspended in torturous pleasure for a few minutes, but it had felt like an eternity to her. And when he finally brought her sweet release—

"Sophie, are you quite well? You've gone the most worrying shade of red."

Sophie shook herself out of her thoughts, shifting uncomfortably in her seat as her sex ached with her memories, and blinked at her sister. "I am well," she lied. "I am simply thinking."

Verity met her confession with a knowing grin, then glanced down the table to Thomas. "She is merely thinking."

"Do let me know if there is anyone I must challenge to a duel," Thomas replied with an equally impish grin before sipping his wine. He stood. "We need to be on our way if we are to arrive in time."

"But the theater won't open for two hours at least," Sophie said.

Verity rose as well. "Of course not, but the cream of society and the dregs will be there to display themselves to each other any time now, and we wouldn't want to miss the show."

In fact, Sophie was certain her sister would be part of the show playing a leading role. She wasn't merely content to enjoy her life as an outcast of the *ton*, she seemed determined to fling her happiness at those who had rejected her at every opportunity.

Sophie had far more clandestine plans to enjoy her newly fallen state. "I might retire early," she said, rising and following her sister and brother-in-law into the hall.

Verity turned to her with a surprised look that quickly melted to teasing suspicion. "Retire early?" she asked.

Sophie shrugged and failed to meet Verity's questioning gaze. "I can retire early now and then without raising the alarm, can't I?"

"You most certainly can," Thomas told her, resting a hand on the small of Verity's back and steering her toward the front door, where Madison stood ready with her evening wrap. "But as I said, let me know if I need to wring someone's neck at any point."

"You won't," Sophie promised, her face as hot as blazes. She wasn't fooling anyone. But odder still, they weren't rushing to warn her of the evils of concupiscence and forbidding her to act upon it. George and his wife, Anne, would have locked her in her room if they knew even half of what she was contemplating, or what she'd done at the banquet.

As soon as Verity and Thomas had left, Sophie fled to the parlor to collect her wits. She considered asking herself if she really wanted to proceed with her plan to give her body and her virtue away to Jonathan, but it was a ridiculous question. She couldn't remember wanting anything more. As glorious as the orgasm he'd sparked in her had been, a tremendous part of her had been disappointed that he didn't follow it by penetrating her and completing the consummation. He'd completed himself on the silk between her legs instead, and while that carried with it a certain kind of eroticism, she'd left the banquet hall feeling empty.

And now, tonight, within a matter of hours, she would be

filled. Her heart pounded as she wondered what Jonathan would want to do with her or what he would want her to do with him. She'd practiced swallowing sausages again at breakfast that morning, but after the glimpse she'd had of his manhood as they'd stiffly untangled themselves from the banquet table, she no longer believed a tiny sausage was adequate. She'd been forced to admit that she had no idea what she was walking into, only that she was desperate for it.

"Miss Sophie." Madison interrupted her thoughts so suddenly that Sophie jumped. "You have a visitor," he went on.

A moment of panic filled Sophie. Jonathan wouldn't come to Thomas and Verity's house, would he? She wasn't sure she could take him up to her bedroom with Madison keeping watch.

"Sophie! How I've missed you!" It was Rebecca who rushed into the parlor, her face pink and her eyes bright.

"Rebecca." With a sudden wave of joy, Sophie rushed to greet her dear friend with a hug. "What are you doing here? How were you allowed to come see me?"

"I snuck out of the house," Rebecca giggled, holding Sophie at arm's length. "Kitty came with me," she said, referring to one of the upstairs maids from Rebecca's home. "I don't have much time, though. You must come with me." She grabbed Sophie's hand and tugged her toward the door.

"Come with you?" Sophie pulled her to a stop by the front door, which Madison stood by, ready to open. "Oh, but I cannot. I...I have an engagement later this evening."

"But you must," Rebecca said, her eyes wider than ever. She sent a covert glance toward Madison. "I have something of grave importance I must tell you. Something I must show you. And if we do not hurry, it will be too late."

"I'm not sure if I can simply—"

"Hurry," Rebecca urged her, pulling her on.

Sophie sighed and stopped resisting. Rebecca lived only one street over, so it wasn't out of the question for her to be able to run and see what Rebecca had to show and to still make it to Jonathan's house on time.

Kitty was waiting on the sidewalk, glancing around nervously. She followed behind as Rebecca dashed along at a swift pace.

"What do you have to show me?" Sophie asked.

"Shh." Rebecca silenced her, glancing over her shoulder to Kitty as they turned a corner and headed on.

Curiosity burned through Sophie as Rebecca drew her down the lane toward the mews instead of along the main street that fronted the line of fashionable, Mayfair townhomes. Rebecca stayed near the shadows as she skittered on, never letting go of Sophie's hand. When they reached the kitchen door at Rebecca's house, they slowed. Rebecca gestured for complete silence, and they slipped into the house.

Kitty stayed in the kitchen, breathing an audible sigh of relief, but Rebecca drew Sophie on. It felt strange to skip through the downstairs halls of someone else's house, but Sophie had to admit that wasn't the strangest thing she'd done lately. They climbed a flight of stairs and headed down a corridor before Rebecca paused at a small, narrow door. She took a key out from a string around her neck and unlocked the door.

"You'll have to go on without me," she whispered. "I told Mama I needed to relieve myself, but she'll be wondering what took me so long."

"But…what am I meant to do? Where does this door lead?" Sophie asked.

"It's a secret corridor," Rebecca whispered. "Follow it until it turns, then move the third panel on the right. You'll be able to see into the room. I'm certain they're still in there."

THE DELECTABLE TART

"But—"

"Shh!" Rebecca held a finger to her lips, then opened the narrow door and pushed Sophie in. "Go."

Sophie had no choice but to obey. She stumbled into the corridor—which was no wider than the span of a man's shoulders—and rested her hands on the walls. It was a good thing she did, for as soon as Rebecca shut the door behind her, Sophie was plunged into pitch black. The only light in the corridor was an occasional peep of light from some kind of intermittent lattice above her head.

As mad as the whole thing was, Sophie moved forward, keeping her hands on the walls as she walked. Anything could be in the corridor, so she moved carefully, sliding her feet in front of her in case the floor suddenly dipped or she ran into stairs. But the floor was smooth and even, and the only breaks in the walls were protrusions that felt like handles of some sort.

She came to an intersection in the corridor, and after a heart-stopping moment of worry that she was lost, she turned right and continued on. Her right hand touched one of the protrusions, and a few yards on, another. She wondered if they could be the panels Rebecca had mentioned.

A few yards farther along, she heard muffled voices from the other side of the wall. Or rather, she heard muffled sounds that were part human, part animal. As her hand touched a third protrusion, she heard a man groan passionately. Sophie's brow shot up. She closed her hand over the handle in the wall, jiggling it, and discovered it might slide up, but she hesitated, uncertain whether to open it in case the people in the room noticed.

"Why did you stop?" the male voice panted. "I'm not there yet."

"I need to catch my breath," a female voice said.

"Catch it quickly," the man snapped. "Or I'll come on your face instead of down your throat."

"All right," the woman said.

Moments later, the man let out an impassioned sigh, but that wasn't what had the hair on the back of Sophie's neck standing on end. She recognized the voices. She would have known them anywhere. It was the man and the woman who had spoken in French right beside her during the banquet. It was the spies.

As carefully as she could with her heart beating wildly in her throat, she slid open the panel in front of her. It only opened an inch, and some sort of thin screen veiled it from inside the room, but it was more than enough to give her a clear view of what was going on in the room.

Lord James Grey leaned against the back of a sofa only ten feet away from Sophie. His breeches were undone and sagging around his knees and his shirt was tucked up around his stomach. Rebecca's sister Mary knelt in front of him, gripping his hips as she jerked back and forth with his cock in her mouth. Her bodice was undone and her breasts swayed free in time with her movements. When Lady Mary rocked back, gasping for breath, Lord Grey's penis popped up, flushed and damp, but far smaller than Sophie thought penises were supposed to be.

"What's taking you so long?" Lady Mary panted.

"I'm nearly there," Lord Grey growled. "Seven Dials whores can finish me off faster than you can."

"Then why haven't you paid one of them for the honor," Lady Mary said bitterly, then caught Lord Grey's member and moved it back to her mouth. She bore down on him at a pace that made Sophie's neck hurt just watching her.

Although watching Lady Mary's dedication as she pleasured Lord Grey tickled something hot and alluring in Sophie. She wondered if Jonathan would like it if she did that to him. Her body warmed, her pulse sped, and her sex ached as she watched Lord Grey's cock sliding in and out of Lady Mary's mouth. She licked her lips, moving a hand up her side to hold her breast.

"Ahh," Lord Grey sighed, tilting his head back and rolling his eyes up. "That's a good girl, that's a good girl." He grabbed her head with both hands and pushed her deeper and faster.

"Have they finished yet?"

Rebecca's whisper at Sophie's side caused her to yelp in shock. A moment later, Lord Grey let out a sacrilegious expletive, followed by a long groan.

"He's finished now," Rebecca giggled. "Lord Grey always takes God's name in vain when he comes. They do this all the time," she went on. "Mary does whatever he tells her to. One time, I caught them with his willy in her bottom and—"

"Rebecca," Lady Mary shouted with a sort of anger that Sophie had never heard before. "I know you're in there."

"Oh no," Rebecca squeaked. "This wasn't supposed to happen." She grabbed Sophie's hand and dashed back through the black corridor so fast that Sophie feared for her life in the dark.

"You brought me here to see your sister fellating Lord Grey?" Sophie gasped as thumps and knocking sounded from the end of the corridor they were fleeing.

"No, I brought you here because Lord Grey—"

Her words were cut off as the far end of the corridor filled suddenly with light.

"So you like the look of your sister's activities, do you, Lady Rebecca?" Lord Grey called after them, out of breath. "I'll treat you to the same as soon as I catch you."

"Dammie," Rebecca gasped, turning the corner. "They've suspected it's me who has been spying on them for some time, but I've managed to prevent them from proving it."

At the word "spying", Sophie's heart dropped to her stomach. "Rebecca, I think they're—"

Another door opened somewhere behind them, and two sets of footsteps echoed in chase.

"Quick, quick," Rebecca shouted.

They shot out the door they'd used to enter the corridor, and with surprising dexterity, Rebecca turned and locked it behind her. As soon as she did, she threw the key down the hall and dashed off in the other direction.

"You need to go," she hissed at Sophie. "They can't chase both of us. You go that way and I'll go this way, and we'll meet up later."

"Rebecca, wait!" Sophie shook her head as her friend ran from her.

"Go, go," Rebecca urged her in a whisper.

"I can't," Sophie squeaked.

Rebecca pushed her down the hall the way they'd entered from the kitchen. "If they find you here, it will be a disaster."

Sophie had to admit it was true. Not only that, she was due at Jonathan's house. "I'll go."

"But wait," Rebecca stopped in the middle of her flight and changed direction. "I have to tell you about—"

"You can tell me later," Sophie silenced her, sprinting toward the servant's stairs. "Go. Save yourself."

Her words held even more truth as a thump sounded on the other side of the door to the secret corridor, followed by angry pounding.

"We know it was you," Lord Grey's voice thundered. "You'll be sorry once I catch you, you little slut."

"Go to your room," Sophie whispered over her shoulder as Rebecca followed her down the stairs and into the servant's hall. "Pretend you were asleep. Anything to throw them off the scent."

"All right. Be safe," Rebecca whispered, then dashed off.

Sophie fled dashing down the hall and through the kitchen. A handful of servants glanced up to see what she was going on about, but none of them seemed interested in getting involved. It gave Sophie the precious seconds she needed to flee out the kitchen door and into the mews.

CHAPTER 5

*J*onathan knit his brow in concentration and applied pressure to the bag of rosewater icing he'd whipped up for practice making sugar roses. He glanced at the sketches he'd obtained in Paris that detailed the work of the renowned French chef, Marie-Antoine Carême, and put his full effort into duplicating the effects. Carême had invented the particular technique for working with sugar that Jonathan used just over a decade before. His work was in the highest demand throughout Europe and graced the tables of royalty. He had even baked and decorated Napoleon Bonaparte's wedding cake. The man was a legend, and Jonathan hoped to duplicate his success.

He squeezed the piping bag gently, placing the icing just so on the disk Carême recommended for crafting lifelike flowers. Jonathan's results were as beautiful as anything in Carême's illustrations. He knew he had the talent to excel as his hero had. But he was well aware that talent only carried one so far. Carême had risen from obscurity and poverty, from working in the kitchens of Paris to being lauded in palaces. Jonathan's father was wealthy and respected, in the Caribbean and in London. But as poor as Carême had been, he still had one thing that Jonathan could never claim. Or rather, Jonathan had a mark that instantly set him at the back of the line. His father was an aristocrat, but his mother had been a slave.

He let out the breath he was holding as he finished his icing rose, then held the confection at arm's length. It was as perfect as he could make it. The soft hints of color he'd added to the sugar mixture gave the petals a warm, pink hue that reminded him sinfully of Sophie's skin.

He grinned and set the completed rose among a pile of others. As long as he lived, he would never forget the delectable curves of Sophie's naked body or the way she looked dusted with sugar. He'd been out and about enough in the past two days to catch the gossip about her that was on the lips of every man who had attended his banquet. He'd listened quietly as Sophie's naked form was described in words that ranged from artistic to carnal. And he agreed with each and every declaration that she was the most erotic thing any of them had seen—so erotic that it bordered on obscene.

He couldn't disagree, but at the same time, not one of the men he'd overheard fantasizing about her in the past two days could hold a candle to the eroticism Sophie had displayed for him alone. His mind conjured up memory after memory of the tension that had coursed through her body as he'd pleasured her, the pleading sounds she'd made in her need for release, or the taste of her dewy flower when it had blossomed under his mouth. The memories were so powerful and distracting that he'd stroked himself to orgasm more times than he could count in the last two days just so that he could relieve himself enough to concentrate on work. Not only did he have shipping and trade business to see to during the day, he had received a few commissions after the banquet, though not as many as he'd hoped.

The clock sitting on the mantel of his workroom chimed nine o'clock, and Jonathan set down the bag of icing. It was well past the hour when evening entertainments began, and Sophie hadn't knocked on his door. There was still a chance that she kept fashionable hours and might appear at midnight or even later, but he didn't believe she was the type. She'd been precisely on time to his banquet, and though he hadn't specified what time she should arrive at his house, surely she would have come already if she was planning to show.

He sighed and moved to the pitcher and washbowl that stood at one end of the counter that lined the far wall of the workroom. He hadn't truly thought she would keep their engagement. Young, innocent women like Sophie didn't make appointments to surrender their bodies to bastard tradesmen like him. He washed his hands and dried them with a wicked grin all the same. He'd been looking forward to tangling with Sophie, their bodies slick with sweat as they explored every inch of each other. She'd surprised him with her bravery at the banquet, and he'd been hoping she would surprise him in other ways. At the very least, she would have taken his mind off his troubles—both confectionary and the losses his father's business was suffering because of the relentless French pirates.

Spies. Jonathan pivoted and leaned against the counter. Sophie had said the word "spies" moments before he'd rendered her senseless with passion. What had she meant by that? The question had occupied him nearly as much as fantasies about her naked and writhing with need under him. Why say such a word at the close of the banquet? It made no sense.

A timid knock sounded at the front door of the shop that

made up the front portion of the ground floor of his house. Hope leapt to life in his chest, and the possibility that it could be Sophie made other things leap as well. He pushed away from the counter, took up the lantern that sat on the edge of the table, and walked from the workroom into the pastry shop.

The moment he was able to make out Sophie's face peeking through the window at the front of the shop, Jonathan smiled. She'd come after all. His heart seemed to pulse in his chest as much as anticipation for the purpose of her visit throbbed in his groin. He ignored the suddenly sentimental feeling that came over him and put on his best, most ravenous grin as he unlocked the door and opened it.

"Good evening, Miss Sophie," he greeted her.

His suave greeting was flattened a moment later as Sophie ran into the shop as though someone were chasing her.

"Quick. Shut the door and lock it. Do you have curtains? They must be closed." She panted as though she'd run all the way there from Mayfair.

Jonathan's spirits sank. "Are you embarrassed to be seen entering my establishment?" he asked with a disappointed frown.

"No," Sophie exclaimed, her nervous fidgeting pausing for a moment. "I would never be embarrassed to be seen with someone as talented as you. It's just that I believe I'm being followed, and after the evening I've had…." She gasped for breath, pressing a hand to her chest. "Please, draw the curtains."

Intrigued, Jonathan set his lantern on the counter and moved to draw the curtains at the front of his shop. He usually chose to keep them at least partially open at night, both to display his work to anyone who might be passing in the night and to demonstrate that there was no cash on hand, therefore the shop wasn't worth breaking into. Not that Soho was rife with thievery the way other parts of London were.

"Thank God," Sophie breathed as soon as the curtains were shut. "I was frightened half out of my wits."

Jonathan returned to her, studying her carefully. "Was a footpad on your tail? If someone was harassing you or wished to do you harm, I'll fight them." The offer came as a surprise, even to himself. He didn't consider himself an aggressive man, but he would have taken on an army for Sophie's sake.

But Sophie shook her head. She swallowed as though forcing herself to calm. "It is a long story," she said. "One that is best told somewhere safe."

"Then come with me."

Jonathan took her hand and led her into the workroom. He didn't stop there, though. He gathered the other lantern that lit the space, handing it to Sophie, then led her up a set of stairs to the heart of his home.

"Is this where you live?" Sophie asked, glancing around as they crossed into the master suite of the small townhome.

"It is," Jonathan answered, setting his lantern on the side table in the suite's front room. "It is humble, compared to my father's house in Mayfair, I know, but I prefer to live above my shop than in the lap of luxury, particularly as I live alone."

He took the second lantern from her and carried it to a pair of sliding doors. With one smooth motion, he opened the doors, revealing his bedroom, and set the lamp on his dressing table. When he turned back to the front room, Sophie was in the middle of turning a circle as she surveyed the furnishings.

"It's beautiful," she said with artless awe. "Yes, it is small, but it seems a perfect size. And I know furnishing like this are not cheap goods."

"No," Jonathan laughed, sauntering toward her. In fact, furnishing the humble space had cost more than purchasing the building in the first place. He might have been practical, but he wasn't a monk. Not by any stretch of the imagination. Which brought him back to Sophie. "Who was chasing you?"

Sophie drew in a breath as though something startled her and spun to face him. "The spies," she said, rushing to meet him in the archway left by the open sliding doors. "I know who they are."

In spite of the warmth of expectation that grew steadily inside of him, Jonathan's pulse quickened. "What spies? What did you mean by 'spies' after the banquet?"

"I heard them," she said, closing the gap between him by grasping his arm. "While I was on display. They stood right beside me, talking in French."

The combination of "Spies" and "French" sent an unexpected flash of anger through him. "Please tell me you speak French."

"I do," Sophie said. "Though they were certain I didn't. They believed they were smarter than you or me. They spoke of passing along information about ships and trade routes to Paris enclosed in sweets that they plan to commission from you."

Jonathan's eyes went wide. He mentally raced through the lists of orders that had been placed in the last two days. There were only a handful, but none of them had seemed unusual.

He blinked as Sophie's words came back to him. "Did you say you know who they are?"

"I do." She tightened her grip on his arm. "It's Lord James Grey and Lady Mary Burgess."

As fast as Jonathan's hopes had risen, they came crashing down. "Lord Grey is a slippery fish. He came within inches of fleecing your brother-in-law, Sebastian, out of his fortune.

Even our Bow Street Runner friend, Nigel Kent, couldn't bring any legal charges against him, even though Grey released the fortune."

"But surely your friend could take action when treason is involved," Sophie said. "Not even the highest members of the peerage can dodge proof of treason."

She was right, but it didn't encourage Jonathan to rush into action. "Are you certain it was them?"

"I'd know their voices anywhere," she said. "I recognized them when they whispered about their plan while staring at me." She gasped, touched a hand to her mouth, and said, "I had no idea such wicked people were gazing at me, lying there like that."

Jonathan grinned before he could stop himself. Half the people who had slathered over Sophie's naked body at the banquet were a hundred times wickeder than Lord Grey, but he would rather she remain in blissful ignorance about that. Then again, the way she blushed as she went on hinted that she wasn't as ignorant as he'd thought.

"Lord Grey has a small cock," she said, her eyes suddenly dancing with mirth. "Lady Mary was on her knees, doing that thing where a woman puts it in her mouth." She burst into giggles.

A burst of lust washed through Jonathan. Whatever she'd seen, Sophie knew about it. She'd witnessed something that would have reduced most high-born ladies to tears, and instead, she was giggling.

"Forgive me," he said, his grin spreading wider as he slid one arm around her side until his hand rested on her back. "I keep assuming you are a blushing innocent, but at every turn you prove me wrong."

"I am innocent," she replied breathlessly, a deep blush splashing her cheeks. "That is to say, the knowledge imparted to me by my sisters and my friend, Rebecca, Lady Mary's sister, far exceeds my experience."

"Does it?" he asked, pulling her closer and studying her lips, remembering their taste.

She nodded uncertainly. "I'm afraid you are the sum total of my experience. But what a glorious experience it was." She was completely breathless by the time she finished speaking. Her chest rose and fell rapidly, her breasts pressing against the fabric of her bodice in an alluring manner.

"How would you like to continue with that experience?" he asked. He was a rake and a villain for taking advantage of her when she was clearly in a restless state, but the brightness in her eyes and the excitement that rippled from her were devastatingly arousing.

She pushed that arousal further when she bit her lip and glanced at him with just a touch of shyness. "Do you promise not to stop this time?" she asked in a small voice.

"I didn't stop last time," he said, brushing his other hand up her side to cradle her breast.

"But you did," she said, her voice softer but her eyes dancing with fire. "You made me feel so good, but you didn't…you didn't…."

"I didn't what?" he asked, enjoying her coy awakening far more than he should have. He wanted to hear her speak the unspeakable aloud.

"You know," she whispered.

"Do I?"

Her breathing was quick, and her nipples were visibly hard beneath the thin fabric of her gown. He couldn't resist brushing the backs of his fingers across one nipple. She gasped and lifted to her toes.

"You erupted on the table," she sighed.

"And?" He arched an eyebrow as he watched her return to the erotic state of need she'd been in during the banquet.

"And I wanted you to erupt inside of me," she admitted.

His heart pounded so hard he was certain she could hear it. Blood and need pumped through him, hardening his cock and making him wish it wasn't constrained in his breeches. "What if you didn't like the way it felt?" he asked.

"I would," she gasped. "I know I would. I ached for it."

"What if I'm too big for you? It might hurt."

"Verity and Honor say it's a good hurt and that it goes away quickly," she said.

She had no idea how wild she was making him with her innocent lust. He had no doubt that she was a virgin, but he'd never known a virgin so hungry for passion in his life.

"What if I impregnate you?" he asked, sliding his hands around her back to pull loose the ties holding her bodice together.

"I don't care," she said, a clear note of pleading in her voice. "A baby would be lovely, but Verity says there are ways to stop it from happening."

Twin jolts of lust and sentiment hit Jonathan, and he paused halfway through peeling off her bodice. He studied Sophie's eyes to be sure she was speaking truthfully, but there wasn't an ounce of deception in her voice. She would have welcomed his child inside of her in spite of who he was, in spite of what that child might look like. And somehow he knew that she wasn't being ignorant or saying what she thought he wanted to hear to convince him to have his way with her. She would gladly carry his child if he put one in her. Which, of course, made him desperate to do just that.

"Would you do to me what you witnessed Lady Mary doing to Grey?" he asked pulling her bodice off her shoulders and over her breasts. When he let it go, her whole gown slithered to the floor.

"I want to," she whispered. "Verity and Honor say they like it, and they've told me how to do it."

Dear heavens, at the rate she was going, he'd come before he could take his cock out. Perhaps it was a blessing that he'd finished himself just a few hours before while thinking about her. He took one of her hands and moved it to cup his stiff, trapped erection, sending unbearable pleasure through him.

"Are you sure?" he asked, grinding against her hand. "As you can see, I'm not small, like Grey."

"No," she said, her voice shaking. "You're not."

"Then don't say you weren't warned."

Sophie ached with anticipation as Jonathan tugged at the lace of her stays. Heat from his unmentionables radiated into her hand. Even through his breeches she could tell that he wasn't exaggerating when he said he was large. He frightened her, but he also thrilled her. As he pulled the lace of her stays all the way out of the last loop and let it fall, she couldn't help but reach for the fastenings of his breeches.

He drew in a surprised breath as she loosened them and pushed them down his hips. His cock sprung up between them, and she rushed to touch it. He was hard and thick, easily as thick as one of the balusters making up the railing of Thomas's grand staircase. She trembled at the thought of fitting him within her. Perhaps it would hurt, but that didn't lessen her need to feel him move within her by a hair.

As she continued to stroke and explore him, he unbuttoned his waistcoat, then pulled it off along with his shirt. As he tossed them aside, he made a deep sound of approval as he glanced down to what her hand was doing. Her fingers were petal pink against the flushed caramel of his staff. She loved the contrast, but she wanted more.

Imitating what she'd seen at Rebecca's house, she dropped to her knees. Her stays slipped off one shoulder and her chemise sagged open as she did. She shimmied out of both, baring her hard-tipped breasts to him. Then she leaned forward, closing a hand around the base of his staff and bringing it to her mouth.

She shivered uncontrollably as she drew him into her mouth. His taste was unique and musky. She tested his tip with her lips, licking the bead of moisture that formed there. Part of her felt as though the act was familiar, but not so familiar that she was confident in what she was doing. She lavished attention on his flared tip, teasing the underside with her tongue and sucking gently, as though eating a candy.

"God above, Sophie," Jonathan exclaimed in a strangled voice. He surprised her by grabbing a fist full of her hair—not unlike what she'd seen Lord Grey do to Lady Mary, but without the coarseness—and urged her to take more of him in. A throbbing thrill went through her as she inched his massive length deeper and deeper into her mouth. He was so thick that her eyes began to water. At the same time, her whole body sizzled with the need to take in more and more of him until she was certain she would choke. There was something so supremely erotic about having his engorged cock deep in her mouth that she moaned at the sensation.

Jonathan pulled back slightly, but only so that he could jerk into her mouth. "So good," he managed to say, his words strangled. He glanced down at her as if memorizing the way she looked with his length thrusting between her lips. "You make me want to be a devil," he panted.

She was on the verge of losing herself in the way he used her when he took a step back. His cock slid out of her mouth, and she gasped for breath, not realizing how badly she needed it. Her breasts hung, heavy and sensitive with her chemise pooled under them, though she was so ready to tear away the rest of her clothes that she could hardly stand it.

"It would be a waste to finish that way," Jonathan said,

pulling her to her feet. "You want me deep in your quim, and you're going to get just that."

He took a moment to remove his shoes and to shuck his breeches entirely. Sophie raced to divest herself of the rest of her clothes as well. She didn't get as far as removing her stockings, but Jonathan didn't seem to care. He scooped her up and carried her to his bed, laying her across the coverlet and spreading her legs so far apart that the muscles in her thighs twinged in protest. She tried to close her legs a bit, but he held them forcefully open.

"No," he told her firmly. "Your body is mine, and I'm going to do what I want with it."

The thrill that coursed through her was ten times stronger than what she'd felt when he positioned her for the banquet. Surrender took on a whole new meaning in her mind. She wanted to be his to shape and mold, and she wanted him to do bad things to her. She wasn't even sure what they could be, just that she wanted him to do things to her that would make the arrogant bitches of the *ton* faint in horror.

"You are a work of art," he said in a hungry voice, positioning himself with his knees between her spread legs and his hands planted on either side of her shoulders. "If I could paint you like this, I would." He lowered himself to kiss her with demanding pressure. "Better still, I would pose you like this on a plinth and stare at you for hours as I pleasured myself. I'd feast my eyes on your soft tits with their nipples like candy-coated almonds."

He shifted to close his mouth over one breast, using his tongue to play with her nipple as if it were a candy he wanted to suck on until it melted. The combination of heat and pressure had Sophie whimpering with need.

He moved one hand down across her belly while keeping his balance with the other. His fingers brushed across the still-smooth flesh of her sex. "I want you like this always," he said. "Nothing to stop you from feeling my touch fully. I want you dripping wet with need to the point where it looks like sugar syrup is pouring from you."

He followed his words by teasing his fingers through the slickness. He took his time, as tender as he was insistent on her arousal. He traced her slit with enough pressure for her to feel it but not enough to bring any kind of release. Then he teased the over-sensitized mound of her clitoris just enough to bring her to the gates of pleasure only to pull away. His fingers delved a bit deeper into her folds, then he toyed with her clit again. Again, he brought her close and then denied her, tracing the quivering outline of her sex. He repeated the torture, bringing her so close she mewled in protest when he denied her again.

His teasing continued as he slipped two fingers inside of her as if testing.

"Please," she begged him, her mind unraveling as the intensity of need within her grew.

"Trust me," he said, sliding his fingers up to brush her clit again. "It will be so much better this way."

He stroked her to the brink before moving away. Sophie thought she would cry, his play was so intense. "I need you," she pleaded. "Inside me. Please."

"What if I walked away?" he asked, touching her, but not enough. "Would you end it yourself or would you do as I say and wait?"

"I would do as you say," she admitted, wild with how much she wanted him and terrified by how badly she needed to submit to his whims.

"Really?" he asked. He leaned forward, caressing her sex with his mouth and brushing his tongue across her clitoris. The sweet torment of pleasure flared to impossible heights, and she was certain she would crash into release at last.

But all too suddenly, he pushed back, climbing off the bed entirely, and leaving her suspended at the breaking point. Sophie moaned in frustration but kept her body positioned exactly as he'd left it. She burned. She ached. She could feel him looking at her that way, spread and exposed and suffering deliciously. She could see him just well enough to see the primal fire in his eyes as he pored over the sight of her.

When he grasped himself and began to stroke, she whimpered with frustration. He was going to finish himself off and leave her wanting. He would deny her and she would be helpless to do anything but writhe with incompletion. It was intoxicating and beautiful and only made her want him inside her ten times as much.

And then, as if she'd proven something to him, he flew to her, mounting the bed and sliding himself home between her legs. She gasped as his tip invaded her, then moaned wildly as he thrust, inch-by-inch, deep into her. The flash of pain she felt as her resistance broke was minimal. The sensation of being filled and opened and plundered deeply was all that she could have asked for and more.

"My Sophie," he sighed, sounding as relieved and impassioned as she was. "My sweet." He began to move mercilessly inside of her, his hips pumping, thrusting deeper and deeper. The sounds he made no longer formed words, but they spoke volumes.

She embraced him with her arms and legs, digging her fingertips into the muscles of his back as he worked both of them into a frenzy. Her body was so primed and ready that she burst into a thundering orgasm that throbbed through her, causing her to call out. It was so much better to squeeze uncontrollably around his thickness, and when he growled and tensed, filling her with a liquid sensation, she was certain she'd died and gone to...perhaps not the heaven she'd been raised with, but wherever it was, she wanted to stay there forever.

All too soon, the intensity of the moment of release gave way to a disjointed feeling of contentment. Jonathan had relaxed to cover her, and she continued to embrace him, reluctant for him to pull out of her. It felt as though they'd been joined body and soul, and she wasn't ready to let go of that feeling yet.

"I don't want to crush you," he said at last, rolling away.

"Please, crush me," she sighed, rolling with him. "My body is yours, after all."

He laughed low in his throat and peeled back the bedcovers so that they could slide between the sheets. "You say that now, but you'll feel differently when you've recovered."

"Will I?" she asked snuggling against him and closing her eyes, prepared to sleep.

He didn't answer, and within moments she wouldn't have heard him if he had. She floated off into sleep, certain beyond a shadow of a doubt that she'd found exactly where she wanted to be.

CHAPTER 6

The moment sleep left Jonathan the next morning, his senses snapped to alertness. Something wasn't right. His bed was too warm. His body was loose with contentment instead of racked with guilt. The hollow sensation that he was so used to the night after he'd taken a woman to his bed was absent.

It took his sleep-hazy mind a moment more to realize the odd feeling was because he wasn't alone. Sophie lay snuggled beside him, her soft, regular breath tickling his shoulder. Her smooth, shapely limbs were tangled with his, and her fragrance surrounded him.

He turned his head just enough to study her, shifting as gently as he could to hold her more fully. She'd stayed with him. Morning had come, and she was still there, asleep in his arms. His pulse quickened, and deep, protective contentment spread through him. He'd never had a problem finding a woman interested in the novelty of being ravished by a mulatto. Among a certain set of the upper class, a romp between the sheets with a man like him was considered a grand adventure. But none of those women had stayed with him through the night. They'd taken what they wanted from him and cast him aside like yesterday's fashion.

Sophie was still with him. She'd come to him the night before and she was still there. In spite of the social danger staying in his bed brought her. He adjusted their positions a little more, wanting to cradle her against him and stroke his hands over her warm body. She fit so well against him, and she'd been so devilishly open to everything he'd done to her the night before. And he hadn't been satisfied with taking her once and being done with her. He'd kissed her awake from the slumber she'd fallen into after their first time so that he could wrap her legs around his waist and take her again. Her pussy had been so tight around his cock that he'd spent inside of her long before he wanted to, which meant that as soon as he'd recovered, he pulled her under him to ravish her a third time.

Each time, she'd sighed and moaned like a Seven Dials strumpet. She'd clasped him with her thighs and dug her nails into his flesh. And she'd come as if her world were blasting apart, even though he'd been unforgivably selfish and remiss in pleasuring her. In short, she'd wanted him, perhaps more than any woman ever had.

The thought touched his heart in a way that was so foreign he writhed in discomfort. It made him hard as well, which was a far more familiar feeling. He knew what to do about that, unlike the throbbing in his chest.

He rolled to his back, bringing Sophie with him, and adjusting her legs so that she straddled him. The movement stirred her from sleep. She drew in a breath and stretched, her silken body wriggling against him and sending his blood pumping.

"Good morning," she drawled at last in a sleepy voice.

"Good morning, my sweet." Jonathan greeted her with a

smile, brushing her golden-brown hair away from her face, then stroking her cheek.

She smiled, and it was as though the sun had split through the clouds. Her smile grew as he brushed his hands down her body, teasing her breasts on the way, until he could take hold of her hips. With a little guidance, he nudged her until the tip of his cock pressed into the hot, slick folds of her sex, then pushed slowly inside of her.

Sophie gasped, and her whole body tensed and strained. Her eyes popped wide for a moment, then her lids dropped to a heavy, sultry look as she caught on to what Jonathan wanted from her. She moved hesitantly at first, bearing down on him with uncertainty, but whether it was because sleep still clouded her mind, letting her body take the lead, or whether she was simply a natural at pleasure, she found a rhythm that was perfect for both of them. She arched her back as she rode him, leaving just enough space for him to close his hands around her ample breasts and play with her nipples.

Their passion play escalated quickly. He was close to coming within minutes, but held himself back as much as he could, waiting for her. He knew he wouldn't have to wait long when her mouth fell open in ecstasy and the cries that escaped from her grew pitched and needy. The vision of her riding him, urgent and hungry and so full of pleasure that it made her wild, was more than Jonathan could withstand. And yet, as he thundered into orgasm just as her cunny started to milk him mercilessly, it was his heart that felt how powerfully she wanted him.

He was mad to fall in love, particularly with a lady, no matter how minor her nobility or how dubious her position in society, but there he was, tumbling headfirst into adoration.

She splayed on top of him as soon as they were both

spent and panting. She was as light as air, and he discovered that he deeply enjoyed the way she covered him. He embraced her, tracing lines up and down her back and sides and counting himself the luckiest man in the world.

"I understand what they are so excited about now," Sophie said as soon as she caught her breath.

"Do you?" he asked, sliding his hands down to her bottom and kneading it.

Sophie propped herself above him enough to smile down at him. "My sisters," she said, mischief glowing in her eyes as she woke up fully. "I understand why they go into such raptures while talking about bedsport."

Jonathan couldn't help but grin up at her with smug satisfaction. "You were a perfect tart last night," he teased her. "And just now. I know whores who ply their trade in the port of Kingston who don't want it as desperately as you do."

His split-second of worry that she'd find his teasing insulting vanished as she burst into giggles, lowering her head so that her hair hid her face for a moment. "I did want it," she admitted, an impish light in her eyes. "And I want more of it. I want you to make me feel like a whore every night."

It was the most outlandish thing a woman had ever said to him, and Jonathan laughed. More than laughed, he circled his arms around her, straining up to kiss her. It wasn't a kiss meant to claim and master either. It was a promise, a way of sharing what was still so new and raw inside of him that he didn't know how to put it into words. He wanted Sophie in his bed, riding his cock raw every night too, but an even deeper part of him wanted more.

"We need breakfast," he said, breaking their kiss at last. "And you need to get home before your sister realizes where you've gone and what you've been doing all night."

"Verity wouldn't mind," she said as they climbed out of

bed and set about gathering their clothes and washing up. "In fact, I'm certain she would encourage my behavior."

Jonathan shook his head as he poured water from the pitcher on his washstand into the bowl. "You and your sisters are the most unusual, incomprehensible family I have ever known. Most well-bred young ladies would pale at the prospect of behaving the way you have."

"I know," Sophie said, sharing his wash water. "And most young ladies will live painfully boring lives while being used as bargaining chips in marriage machinations. I am quite content to parcel out my favors to a man who wants me for myself and not the connections I can bring him."

Her comment stuck with him as they finished cleaning up, dressed, and headed downstairs to the kitchen attached to his workroom. His assistants would arrive to open the shop in less than an hour. In fact, Freddy was already there—and likely had been since before they woke up—preparing the basic pastry dough for the day's treats. And yet, Sophie didn't seem to mind. She greeted Freddy with a smile and stood at the stove with Jonathan as he cooked eggs and rashers of bacon.

"Does your sweet shop do a fair amount of business?" she asked as they sat at the kitchen table eating.

"Fair enough," Jonathan said with a shrug. "Though I would like it to do more."

"But your primary business is your father's sugar company, correct?" Before Jonathan could answer with his desire to make confectionary his primary business, she raced on with, "The spies! We nearly forgot about the spies."

Everything he had been about to say, along with his happy, sated mood, vanished. "You know who they are," he said, recalling the details that had emerged from the night before. "Lord Grey and Lady Mary Burgess."

"Yes," Sophie lowered her voice to a whisper, leaning

across the corner of the table to speak to him in hushed tones. "I would be willing to wager Lord Grey is spying for the money it brings him. My sisters' husbands have both run into difficulties with Lord Grey and money."

"He's an earl, is he not?" Jonathan asked with a confused shake of his head. "Does he need money?"

"He's in dire need of it," Sophie went on, peeking sideways at Freddy as he filled pastry shells in the other room. "He cannot stop himself from gambling and he has lost every penny he had and more."

"That would be motivation to turn traitor," Jonathan agreed, stroking his chin. He frowned, thinking over the situation and seeking to find a way to keep Sophie safe in the midst of it. "We need to pay a call on my friend, Nigel."

"The Bow Street Runner?" Sophie asked.

Jonathan smiled. "You remember."

"Of course I remember," Sophie said. "I remember everything you say."

It was silly to let something so sentimental affect him, but Jonathan's heart swelled until it felt too big for his chest. "We'll go to Bow Street right away. Nigel has been hungry to slip a noose around Lord Grey's neck since he found out how close the man came to cheating Sebastian out of his fortune."

Half an hour later, Jonathan and Sophie were seated in the back of a hansom cab, winding their way through London to Bow Street. The Magistrate's Court had barely opened its doors by the time they arrived, but unsurprisingly, Nigel was already there and hard at work.

"Jonathan," Nigel greeted him with a slap on the back. Nigel was so large and strong that he nearly knocked Jonathan sideways with the gesture. "What brings you here so early, and with such fetching company?" He smiled at Sophie.

Sophie's eyes went wide as she took in the sight of Nigel, all six and a half feet of him. She inched closer to Jonathan's side, grasping for his hand. A paradoxical sense of pride filled Jonathan as he took her hand and held it close. Nigel was the gentlest man imaginable…unless he was chasing down a criminal.

"We have information about the spies who are passing shipping and trade secrets to the French," Jonathan said in a low voice. "In fact, Sophie swears she knows their identities beyond a shadow of a doubt."

Nigel instantly tensed in excitement, a hungry grin coming to his lips. "This way," he said, leading them down the court's main hall to a series of offices. He threw open the door to one of the offices, gestured for Jonathan and Sophie to enter, then shut the door behind them once they were alone. "What do you know?" he asked Sophie.

Sophie stood so close to Jonathan that it would have been easier for him to wrap his arm around her than simply to hold her hand, but she held her head up and said, "It's Lord James Grey and Lady Mary Burgess."

Nigel's brow shot up. "Do you have proof?" he asked, a distinct menace to his voice.

Sophie squeezed Jonathan's hand tighter, but nodded as though she was determined not to be afraid. "At Jonathan's banquet a few days ago. I overheard them plotting to pass slips of papers to their contact in Paris. Slips of paper concealed in sweets and cakes."

Nigel crossed his arms and stroked his chin. "And they said this," he said, not obviously doubting, but clearly attempting to make sure the story was plausible. "Right in front of you. In the middle of a crowded room."

Sophie's cheeks flushed a shade of pink that stirred Jonathan's blood and lowered her eyes slightly. "They didn't know I was there. No one knew I was there, even though I was in plain sight."

Nigel's frown deepened for a moment before he burst into a sudden, wide grin. "That was you, wasn't it?" he asked. "The Delectable Tart."

"I beg your pardon?" Sophie squeaked.

"The decoration," Nigel went on laughing. "You were naked and spread out like some erotic goddess covered in sugar. People have been referring to you as The Delectable Tart."

"That was her," Jonathan answered as Sophie squeaked and clapped a hand to her mouth. He couldn't tell if she was upset by the revelation that she now had a nickname—or possibly that Nigel had seen her in all her sensual glory—or if she was amused by it. Instinct told him it was a bit of both. "Her face was covered and Lord Grey and Lady Mary were speaking in French."

"Which I am fluent in," Sophie added. "They were explicit in their plans. I have no doubt that they are the spies."

"But your face was covered," Nigel said. "If they couldn't see who you were, how did you recognize them?"

"I know their voices," Sophie said. "And though I could not place them at the time, last night I was…." She paused, her face turning redder. "I was in a position to observe Lord Grey and Lady Mary alone together. I knew at once what I heard at the banquet, that they are the spies."

"Interesting," Nigel said, returning to rubbing his chin. "I would give my left nut to bring Lord Grey to justice," he growled. But then he sighed. "I won't be able to act on this evidence alone, though. I would need firm, physical proof of treason."

"What do you need?" Jonathan asked. "We'll find a way to get it for you."

"Documentation," Nigel said with a shrug. "Proof of their

French contacts. It would be most effective if they were caught in the act."

Jonathan's shoulders sagged. It was unlikely any of them would be in a position to obtain the kind of proof Nigel needed. The circles of high society were closed to all three of them.

But Sophie merely smiled at the problem and said, "That should be easy enough."

Both Jonathan and Nigel looked askance at her.

She went on. "Lord Grey and Lady Mary plan to pass secrets to the French enclosed in cakes. But they need to do it discreetly."

"Obviously," Nigel said.

"Perhaps at an event where a large amount of cakes will already be present?" Sophie practically glowed with mischief. "Especially if they received urgent, new information that needed to be transferred immediately?"

Jonathan and Nigel exchanged confused glances.

"I suppose I could host another banquet," Jonathan said. "Though I'm still recovering from the expense of the first one. It might take a month to set up."

"A month is not soon enough," Nigel said. "If these two have any sense their identities have been uncovered, they will stop at nothing to hide their wrongdoing. And besides, we don't have the sort of shipping information they would be interested in."

"Sebastian would," Sophie said, still looking as though she knew things they didn't. "And even if he doesn't, he could make something up and have his solicitor, Mr. Proctor, pass it along somehow."

"That doesn't solve the problem of providing Lord Grey with a situation in which he could convey the information," Nigel said.

Sophie clucked and shook her head. "Have neither of you been mindful of the events of the *ton* this spring?"

Jonathan and Nigel exchanged a glance as if it were ridiculous for them to know anything about the *ton*.

Sophie shook her head and went on. "Lady Charlotte Grey has just become engaged to Lord Gosford. Their engagement ball will be held Thursday next."

A slow grin spread across Jonathan's face. A moment later, Nigel seemed to catch on.

"Do you know who is providing the refreshments for the party?" Nigel asked.

"I don't, but I could find out," Jonathan said.

"The Greys employ a small army of their own cooks," Sophie said. "But according to Verity, the servants have no great love of their masters. If an important Bow Street Runner spoke to their butler and cook, I'm certain the staff would be amenable to assisting the efforts of the law in bringing traitors to justice."

Jonathan's spirits rose higher. "It would be as easy as Sophie says to infiltrate the house if that is true. I could construct cakes that beg for secrets to be passed within them."

"We could catch them in the act," Nigel said, his grin wolfish. He ground one meaty fist into his other palm. "This would be exactly the sort of case that would prove the importance of having a more organized, more permanent policing force in the city," he said.

"I, for one, would love to see Lady Mary brought to justice," Sophie said, tilting her head up with a look of disdain. "That would teach her to forbid me to be friends with Rebecca."

Jonathan couldn't help but smile at her determination. In so many ways, Sophie was a strong and sensual woman, but she wasn't as far removed from the schoolroom as all that.

Then again, when Jonathan thought of people like Nigel and Sebastian, he understood fully that there was nothing so important as a good and faithful friend.

"We should get to work making plans as soon as possible," he said, taking Sophie's hand.

"I'll send someone around to speak to Lord Grey's butler to see if his staff is open to the scheme," Nigel said. "I'll be in touch."

"This is so exciting," Sophie said a few minutes later as they stepped back into the street. "I feel as though we might truly be able to do some good."

"If we can bring spies to justice, then of course we will do good," Jonathan agreed. He held Sophie's arm and gazed at her, an unaccountable joy filling him. If they hadn't been standing in the middle of a busy sidewalk, he would have kissed her.

He leaned closer to her, debating throwing caution to the wind and kissing her anyhow, but a flicker of movement caught the corner of his eye. He straightened and turned in the direction he thought the movement had come from, but nothing was there.

"We should hail a cab and be on our way," he said, frowning.

"What is it?" Sophie asked, glancing this way and that. "Are we still being followed?"

Jonathan blinked at her. "You felt it too?"

Her expression turned worried. "Whoever was following me last night must still be following me this morning."

Jonathan reached out to hail a cab, and fortunately, one pulled alongside them in short order. "Do you know who it could be?" he asked.

"It must be Lord Grey and Lady Mary," Sophie whispered. "Or someone associated with them. Lord Grey was not happy that Rebecca was spying on him and Lady Mary from the secret corridor last night. He must have discovered that I was with Rebecca somehow."

A thousand warning bells sounded in Jonathan's head at her strange statement, but he didn't have time to address any of them as he handed Sophie up into the carriage. "So Lord Grey didn't see you?" he asked once they were seated and the driver was given directions to Lord Landsbury's house in Mayfair.

"No," Sophie said, her brow knitting in confusion. "But the servants in the kitchen did. Lord Grey must know I was there."

"Then we need to get you home as soon as possible," Jonathan said. "I couldn't bear it if anything happened to you."

CHAPTER 7

Sophie could hardly believe how exciting her life had become in such a short time. She'd thought the world was coming to an end when Verity and Honor were cast out of society, but now she was certain that the life she had known before was only a tiny sliver of everything there was to experience. And while she was fully aware that the things she'd done in the past several days were horrifically wicked and scandalous, it felt as though they had brought her back to life.

"It's early still," she told Jonathan as the cab rolled to a stop in front of Landsbury House. "Verity and Thomas were out at the theater last night, which means they would have returned home at a ridiculous hour. I believe they won't be out of bed before noon." She was relatively certain that they wouldn't spend all that time asleep, though.

"Are you saying you want me to come in?" Jonathan asked as he helped her down from the carriage.

Sophie blinked at him, suddenly anxious that he was bored of her at last. "If you'd like to," she said. "We have so much to discuss. Our trap needs careful planning before it's set." She glanced sideways at the driver, not wanting to say too much in front of him.

For a moment, Jonathan merely stared at her, studying her with an unreadable look. At least it wasn't a look of disapproval. If she had to venture, Sophie would have called it bafflement, as if he'd discovered something good that he hadn't expected to be there. He turned away all too soon to pay the driver.

That was when Sophie noticed a dark carriage at the far end of the street. It pulled into the intersection a few dozen yards away, slowed almost to the point of stopping, then suddenly drove on. It was as if whoever was in the unmarked vehicle wanted to see for themselves that Sophie and Jonathan had arrived, but didn't want to make it obvious that they'd been following.

"We need to get inside quickly," Sophie whispered as Jonathan and the driver exchanged final pleasantries.

"Is something wrong?" Jonathan asked, taking Sophie's arm and escorting her from the cab to the front steps of Landsbury House.

"Our shadows," she whispered as Madison opened the door.

"Good morning, Miss Sophie." Madison bowed as she and Jonathan swept into the house. "I am relieved to see you've returned safely at last."

Sophie winced, feeling a pinch of guilt. "I'm sorry I failed to mention I would be out all night. I…I wasn't sure myself how the evening would unfold." She glanced to Jonathan and blushed.

Madison stood stiffly and surveyed Jonathan with a paternal look. "As long as you are safe and in good hands, miss."

Sophie smiled from ear to ear. That was as close to approval as she was likely to get from Madison.

"Will you be requiring repast, Miss Sophie?" Madison asked on.

"No, we've eaten, thank you, Madison," Sophie said, grabbing Jonathan's hand and leading him to the stairs.

Jonathan's brow shot up. "Where are we going?" he asked.

"Somewhere we can discuss our plans in secret," she whispered, excited all over again.

"Upstairs?" Jonathan sent an apologetic glance to Madison, but followed Sophie up to the first floor all the same.

"Our shadow might listen at the window if we stay downstairs," she said, though if she were honest with herself, that wasn't her entire reason for tugging Jonathan along the hall to her cozy bedroom.

As soon as she'd whisked him inside and shut the door behind them, she breathed a sigh of relief.

"Now," she said, crossing the room to her wardrobe. "What can we do to ensure Lord Grey and Lady Mary will attempt to pass secrets to the French during Lady Charlotte's engagement party?" She pulled the ties of her gown loose.

When Jonathan didn't immediately answer, she turned to see what had him so silent. He stood in the middle of her room with his arms crossed and a wry grin on his handsome face.

"Is there a problem?" she asked, her stomach fluttering with worry.

"What are you doing?" he asked, shaking his head.

"Removing my soiled clothes," she said, baffled that she had to explain.

"With me standing right here?" he asked.

Sophie smiled and let out a brief laugh. "It's not as though you've never seen me undressed before," she said, continuing to remove her gown. "I dare say you've seen me more undressed than anyone ever has."

"I have," he agreed. "And every time has left me hard as

iron, without the faculties of thought, and desperate to sink myself into you to the hilt."

"Has it?" she asked, feeling her face heat. She stepped out of her gown and draped it over the back of a chair, then set to work on her stays. "And how is it making you feel now?"

He answered by drawing in a deep, ragged breath and working open the buttons of his jacket. "Like I would be unforgivably rude to continue on fully clothed while you bare yourself to me."

Her cheeks burned hotter. "What if I like baring myself to you?" she asked, freeing her stays and shrugging out of them. She started slowly peeling away the layers of her underthings. "What if I enjoy the sensation of being observed in the state nature intended?"

"Do you?" he asked, removing his jacket and crossing to drape it over the chair where she'd placed her gown. "Do you like to be looked at?"

Sophie bit her lip and nodded, then drew her chemise—the last of her clothes save her stockings—over her head. "I find it invigorating," she confessed.

"Even when you know what men are thinking as they gaze upon you?" he asked, slipping out of his waistcoat.

"Yes," Sophie said. She plucked at the ribbons holding her stockings up, then pulled them off and moved toward her bed. "I want to do it again," she said, leaning back against the copious number of pillows at the head of the bed, arms above her head, legs parted. "I want people to look at me like this and to be stirred with lust."

Jonathan yanked off his boots and tugged his shirt free from his breeches, then advanced toward her. "I'm not certain I want half the men of London slathering over you," he said.

"Ah, but slathering is all they will get," she said, resting one arm on her headboard while slowly drawing the other from her cheek to her neck and across her breast and down. "You are the only one who will consume The Delectable Tart at the end of the evening," she finished, teasing her fingers across the bare flesh of her sex.

"You truly are a shameless hussy," he laughed, though there was more hunger than teasing in his eyes. "Would you have a crowd of men watch you treat yourself thusly?" He nodded to where she was still caressing herself with a feather-light touch.

A rush of excitement coursed through her at the thought, and instead of light strokes, she slipped her fingers deeper into her folds. An intense rush of pleasure filled her as she fingered the bundle of her clitoris. Jonathan's gaze grew ravenous as he watched her, and the bulge in his breeches stood out noticeably. That only served to arouse her more. She could bring him pleasure without even touching him, which meant she could do the same for a room full of men if she wished.

The thought delighted her while at the same time made her feel shockingly wicked. She was horrified at herself, but she was also aching and wet at the thought.

"Are you ashamed of me for wanting men to look at me?" she asked in a small voice.

Jonathan took a moment to answer. The carnal look in his eyes softened to a sort of understanding. "We all have things within us that defy the rules and expectations," he said. "And I would be a hypocrite if I said I didn't want people feasting on the sight of you, because I ache to dust you with sugar and use you as a canvas for my work again."

"You do?" Her heart and her hopes lifted. She didn't feel quite so evil with his thoughts in accord with hers. "I would like that."

He moved closer to her, grasping her waist and pulling her farther down the bed. He began to arrange her limbs in an erotic pose the way he had before. "My father's business has made me wealthy beyond anything the son of a slave could have imagined, but my dreams have a sweeter taste." He spread her legs farther, brushing his fingers across her inner thighs as though icing them with intricate designs. "I want to make a name for myself as a confectioner. I want to make the mouths of the high and mighty water as they look upon my work. I can see that happening with you as the focus of my art."

"I will do anything you ask me to do," she said, her breath coming in shallow gasps.

Jonathan leaned closer to her legs. "I see a row of miniature tarts lined up here," he said, kissing the tingling skin just above her knee. "I see royalty vying with each other to pluck each sweet in turn." He kissed her thigh a few more times, making a trail up to her sex. "I see men fighting each other to pay the cost of eating the cake that forms the center of the design." His kisses reached the apex of her thigh, and Sophie was dizzy from holding her breath and keeping still. "The cake that would rest right here."

He drew his tongue across her dewy opening, causing her to gasp and shiver with delight. His lips worked magic on hers, and his tongue teased her with the promise of ecstasy.

"You wouldn't let them do this, would you?" she managed to ask through shallow pants.

"Never," he said, glancing up from between her legs with a glint of mischief in his eyes. "But I would make them think they could."

"That would be dangerous," Sophie mewled, feeling herself speeding toward orgasm. "Powerful men believe they can take what they want whenever they want it."

"You make me feel more powerful than all the kings of the world combined," he said, then doubled the efforts of his lips and tongue.

Sophie burst into orgasm with a bone-deep sigh of pleasure. She reveled in the way her body throbbed and shuddered, grasping for as much pleasure as she could handle and more. She didn't know how so many of the women who called themselves respectable and reputable could live without such wonder. And they considered themselves to be superior in every way. How wrong they were.

Jonathan rocked back as her orgasm subsided, rushing to remove his shirt and breeches. Sophie was already breathing heavily when he stood and shucked his breeches and stockings entirely, but her heart raced anew at the sight of his thick penis striving up in readiness. They'd been so active the night before that she was sore, but that didn't stop her from wanting him inside her once again.

"My sweet," he rumbled, kneeling between her legs. He surprised her by lifting her to sit, then maneuvering her so that she faced away from him. It all made sense when he shifted her toward the mound of pillows and her headboard and positioned himself as a protective cage behind her, his arms around her. "Say you'll be mine, that you'll be my art and my muse."

He lifted her hips and found her entrance, sheathing his cock slowly inside of her. Sophie gasped, and her mouth stayed open at the glorious sensation of their odd angle of coupling. She grasped the edge of her headboard with both hands as he moved impossibly deep inside of her. She didn't think she could take so much of him, but her body blossomed around him.

"Yes," she moaned, in answer to his question and in response to his increasing thrusts.

He shifted their position slightly, nudging her knees wider and bending her forward until her breasts sagged heavily, jostling as he picked up his pace. "Say you'll stay with me, making my dreams a reality."

"Yes," she gasped. Whether it was his dreams to achieve fame for his sweets or simply his dream to possess her in every wicked way, she wanted nothing more than to be his. Her body, heart, and soul were in agreement, and she cried out with pleasure as he claimed her.

The power of his thrusts was almost punishing. If he were a lesser man, she would have felt used and violated by the way he took her so thoroughly. His cock stretched her to the limit, filling every bit of her to breaking, and yet, even with the soreness from the night before, it was glorious. She submitted to him, giving in to his need and allowing her body to be a vessel for his pleasure.

He moved his hands from her hips to cradle her breasts as the tell-tale sounds he made hinted he was close to release. Her own body felt as though it was coiling tighter and tighter around him, ready to explode into bliss once more. Her knuckles were white on her headboard as she jerked her hips along with his thrusts, trying to take more of him than was possible. And when he pinched her swollen and aching nipples, she screamed in pleasure as her body tumbled into an orgasm so strong she thought it would drive her mad.

Her pussy squeezed around him, and with a triumphant groan from Jonathan, warmth spread into her. His thrusts grew suddenly heavy, and a moment later, his hands returned to grip her waist as he sagged over her. He held himself inside of her as she braced herself against the headboard, reveling in every moment of it.

"This pose would turn heads," she gasped at last, imagining the shock of the *ton* if they could see the two of them in such a carnal embrace.

A moment later, Jonathan's panting turned into laughter. "I believe there are performances of the like in Paris," he said, slowly disengaging from her, flopping to his back, and bringing her with him. "Some people would rather watch than participate."

"France is such a wicked place," Sophie giggled, still trying to catch her breath. She felt fresh and rejuvenated now that the intensity of their mating was over and nestled against him in complete contentment.

"It most certainly is," Jonathan agreed. "Though London has its share of vice as well."

"If you truly wish to pursue the idea of displaying me as your confection, we would become a part of the center of that vice," she said, uncertain how she felt about it. She lifted herself enough to look down at him. "Are you certain that's what you want?"

"I will be honest," he said, rubbing a hand across his damp face and heavy-lidded eyes. "I can't think one way or another about it at this moment."

She grinned, finding that somehow endearing. Her mind was much clearer, though. "Would you be content to become London's premier provider of erotic treats instead of simply a renowned pastry chef?" she asked. "Because I think you could become the former with the greatest of ease, whereas the latter…."

She let her words fade as she played with the damp hair on his chest. His maple brown chest. The challenges he would face in the haughty society she'd been raised in would be made a hundred times worse by the fact of his birth, but the secret side of society, the world of sin and danger, was far more open to difference. She'd learned that in the months since her sisters' disaster at Almack's more than anything else.

Jonathan glanced up at her, brushing the back of his fingers across her hot cheek and studying her with a look of intense consideration. Sophie wanted nothing more than to hold him and make things as wonderful for him as he had made them from her, whatever that meant.

She leaned down to kiss him, then said, "You don't have to decide—"

A knock at her door shocked her to silence. Her body tensed almost painfully, and she huddled close to Jonathan.

"Miss Sophie," Madison said, then cleared his throat.

Sophie's face went hot all over again, this time with acute embarrassment. She realized after the fact how loud she and Jonathan had been.

"Miss Sophie?" Madison asked once more.

"Yes, Madison?" Sophie called as she squirmed her way off the bed, searching for her robe.

"Forgive the interruption," Madison went on, "but you have a visitor."

CHAPTER 8

*J*onathan cringed at the butler's announcement and leapt off of Sophie's bed, his drained energy instantly restored. He'd known exactly what following Sophie to her bedroom would lead to. He should have been wise enough to stop himself. But where Sophie was concerned, he had shamelessly little control.

"Er, tell my guest I shall be down directly," Sophie called through the door, scampering toward her wardrobe, then changing her mind and rushing to her washstand. "I just need to…er…freshen up first."

"Yes, miss," the butler said. His retreating footsteps creaked down the hall.

"I'm sorry," Jonathan said, joining Sophie at the washstand to clean up as best he could. "I shouldn't have let things go so far."

Sophie laughed and paused her ablutions to lift to her toes and kiss his cheek. "I think it's only fair for me to take responsibility for starting things." She kissed his cheek a second time. "But we must hurry. There is no telling who awaits me downstairs."

Jonathan agreed and raced through dressing. It was far more complex to dress carefully enough not to look as though they'd just had a satisfying romp than it was to divest themselves of clothing, and he felt each tick of the clock as he fastened his breeches, tucked his shirt in, and tied his cravat. Sophie had just as much trouble as she donned entirely fresh clothes, from chemise and stockings all the way to the attractive, blue gown she took from her wardrobe. He helped her with the ties in back and she helped him with the buttons of his waistcoat. Somewhere behind the urgency of knowing someone was waiting on them, Jonathan found himself delighting in the way they took such care with each other. It was almost as though they functioned as well together out of bed as they did in.

All the same, he had no intention of embarrassing Sophie by being seen coming downstairs with her by whatever guest had come to call. He held back on the stairs, intending to wait until she was ensconced in the parlor with her guest, then rushing out the front door before being seen.

"You don't have to go," she whispered to him as they neared the bottom of the stairs. "I'm certain whoever it is wouldn't mind meeting you."

"I cannot importune you that way, my sweet," he said, cradling her face and kissing her forehead. "It would raise too many questions. I should go."

She glanced up at him with eyes suddenly filled with sadness. "Can I come to your shop later?" she asked. "I want to help you with—"

"Good gracious, is that what has taken you so long to come down to me?" Rebecca asked from the doorway to the parlor.

A sharp, guilty sensation prickled along Jonathan's skin. He'd been caught in spite of his best efforts to spare Sophie humiliation.

"Rebecca," Sophie exclaimed, turning away from him to greet her friend. "What in heaven's name are you doing here?"

"I've been following you since last night," Rebecca said with a long-suffering sigh, clasping a hand to her chest. "Gracious, but you led me a merry chase."

Jonathan studied the young woman with a sense of disbelief mingled with concerned. In fact, Rebecca did look worse for wear. Her gown was creased and her hair was falling out of what might have once been a careful style. She had dark circles under her eyes as well, as if she hadn't slept all night.

"You've been the one following us?" Sophie asked, taking her friend's arm and leading her into the parlor. "Madison, tea for—oh, I see you already have some." Sophie stopped at the sight of a small tea service on a table in the parlor. Jonathan abandoned his plans to leave and followed the two women into the room.

"I will bring more, miss," Madison said from his position of alertness in the hall.

Jonathan nodded to the older man. It was a ridiculous gesture, but it was all he could think to do in the awkward situation.

"I've been following you almost from the moment we ran from Mary and Lord Grey," Rebecca said, sitting on a sofa with Sophie at her side. "I would have run away with you, but I had to find Mama and make an excuse for going to bed."

"Did your mother believe your excuse?" Jonathan asked with a skeptical frown.

Rebecca heaved a sigh. "She might have last night, but if they've discovered me missing this morning, no doubt they will turn London upside down searching for me."

"Then we need to take you home at once," Sophie insisted, attempting to stand and bring Rebecca with her.

"No, not yet." Rebecca caught her arm and urged her to sit.

Jonathan moved to a chair that sat near the sofa, taking a seat with a frown. "How did you follow Sophie last night?" he asked. "How did you trail us here?"

"Randolph," Rebecca said. "Our driver. He helped me escape Mary and Lord Grey last night. He knew to follow Sophie to your shop, Mr. Foster."

Jonathan exchanged a look of surprise with Sophie. He never would have guessed that a young woman from Rebecca's background would have the first idea who he was.

"Randolph has a bit of a *tendre* for me," Rebecca went on, blushing. "He's always said he is devoted to me and would do whatever I asked him to. He waited with me all night in the carriage outside of your shop, then he took me to that ominous, grey building where you went earlier, and then he brought me here. But that's not what I need to tell you," she rushed on as Sophie opened her mouth, likely to ask a question.

"My sister Mary and Lord Grey are spies," Rebecca announced, eyes wide, her cheeks flushing pink.

Jonathan and Sophie merely stared back at her. "Yes, we know," Sophie said.

"Oh." Rebecca's shoulders dropped, and she suddenly seemed every bit as exhausted as someone who had stayed up all night, rushing through town. A moment later, her brow knit in confusion. "But how did you know?"

Sophie glanced to Jonathan, biting her lip. She seemed to be asking permission to reveal all. There didn't seem to be any harm in bringing Rebecca into their confidence, especially when she already knew the identity of the spies, so he nodded.

Sophie let out a breath, grabbed her friend's hands, and rushed into, "I overheard them plotting to pass secrets to their French contact the other day while I was disguised as a centerpiece for Jonathan's confectionary banquet."

She blurted the whole thing as though revealing a major coup, but it was Rebecca's turn to stare blankly instead of gasping in surprise.

"You were disguised as a centerpiece?" Rebecca asked dubiously.

"I was completely naked," Sophie giggled. "And Jonathan sprinkled me with sugar and covered my body with icing and marzipan and cakes. It was positively decadent, and half the *ton* observed me without knowing who I was. My face was hidden by silk, you see."

Rebecca's eyes went wide and she clapped a hand to her mouth. Jonathan shifted in his chair, fighting the awkward sensation that the two women were barely more than girls in short skirts gossiping about scandals. Considering what he'd been doing with Sophie not half an hour before, it made him feel like the lowest rake imaginable. He had to remind himself that Sophie was comfortably in her twenties, regardless of how sheltered and controlled her life had been before.

"People saw you without clothes?" Rebecca squeaked. "On purpose?"

"Yes, and it was delicious," Sophie said. She stopped and sat straighter as if she'd had a sudden thought. "But how did you know Mary and Lord Grey are spies?"

"I've heard them talk about it," Rebecca said, speaking slowly at first, still visibly shaken by Sophie's revelation. "From the secret corridor," she went on. Her cheeks went from pink to red. "I…well…that wasn't the first time I've been caught spying on Mary and Lord Grey when they are secluded. Mostly they do the sort of things that we saw them doing last night. But sometimes they talk openly because they think no one can hear them. They were discussing plans to pass shipping information along to a Monsieur Langlais, a

Monsieur Rene Langlais, who apparently wants to give them twenty thousand pounds."

Sophie gasped as though watching a drama unfold on stage, but Jonathan's gut hardened in rage. So that was the name of the French contact who was decimating British shipping. For his father's sake and for the sake of his friends, Jonathan wanted to find Langlais and wring his neck.

"We need to take this information to Nigel as soon as possible," he said. "This is information he can act upon."

"We shouldn't take it to any Nigels," Rebecca said, twisting to face Jonathan. "We should take it to parliament or a constable or a Bow Street Runner."

"Nigel is a Bow Street Runner," Sophie said. "That's what the ominous building you followed us to this morning was."

"The Bow Street Magistrate's Court," Jonathan said. "We need to go back there immediately." He rose.

"There isn't time," Rebecca said, though she stood when Sophie did. "Wouldn't the Bow Street people have to begin a new investigation and search for evidence? That takes ages. I overheard Mary and Lord Grey's entire plot, and it requires action now. They have the information, and they plan to pass it along to the Frenchman at Lady Charlotte's engagement party on Thursday."

"I knew it," Sophie shouted in triumph. "When they were standing over me at the banquet they spoke of concealing the secrets in cakes. What better opportunity would they have to commission a large quantity of cakes and to have a host of guests in their house without raising questions than at Lady Charlotte's engagement party?"

Jonathan grinned at Sophie's excitement, and at her intelligence. Though he was still caught between thinking she was brilliant for puzzling the whole thing out and thinking Lord Grey and Lady Mary were unforgivably stupid for passing secrets so openly. There was a fair chance they hadn't been in the business of spying for long, though, and from what Jonathan knew of Lord Grey's desperate need for funds, the man was likely favoring speed over caution in securing his money.

"There is time to foil the plot," Jonathan assured Rebecca. "My friend, Mr. Nigel Kent, has already been investigating Lord Grey. I believe he is prepared to act by the party on Thursday. For now, you need to go home before your parents raise the alarm."

"I want to help," Rebecca said, flying to him and grasping his arm. She seemed to notice what she'd done a moment later and pulled away as though Jonathan were made of fire. She lowered her head sheepishly and said, "That is to say, I want to see my sister and Lord Grey brought to justice."

"But she's your sister," Sophie said, crossing to join them. "If she is caught by the Bow Street Runners and found guilty, it could mean death." She whispered the last word as the color drained from her face. The full implication of everything they were involved in must have struck her at last.

"Sophie is correct," Jonathan said. "If Grey and your sister are caught, they will hang. Perhaps your assistance would be better served advising your sister to stay away from Lord Grey from here on out."

Rebecca shook her head, standing straighter. "Mary is a wicked woman," she said. "She's done scandalous things and gotten away with them. She's hurt people. She hurt me by forbidding me to continue my dearest friendship with Sophie. But I...I do not want to see her hang," she went on hesitantly. "All the same she should be brought to justice. I want to help." She nodded in affirmation of her original statement.

Jonathan rubbed a hand over his face. They needed to take their conversation to Nigel. He was in over his head and well aware of it. "I promise you," he told Rebecca, "we will involve you in whatever we decide to do. But it is imperative that you return home so that your parents do not suffer more worry than necessary."

"And if they catch you out they may forbid you from attending Lady Charlotte's party altogether," Sophie said.

A burst of frustration hit Jonathan. It was a travesty to see women treated as children. Perhaps it was no surprise at all that Sophie was so enthusiastic about doing things that would make other women expire from shame. The freedom she must have felt by being wicked would be intoxicating after a stifling life of insignificance.

"I'll go home," Rebecca said with a disappointed sigh. "You are right about Mama's fury. And I must be at Lady Charlotte's engagement party. You must come up with a way for me to participate in the plot to catch Mary and Lord Grey. I'll do anything."

"Anything?" Sophie asked, one brow inching up. Jonathan had a sinking feeling she had something in mind.

"Anything," Rebecca said with passion.

Jonathan couldn't help but grin. He had a feeling he and Nigel would have their hands full as they executed a plan to catch the spies at last.

Sophie was amazed by how swiftly everything moved once she and Jonathan returned to Bow Street to explain Rebecca's revelations to Nigel Kent. As it happened, Nigel and his colleagues were already aware of Monsieur Rene Langlais. The man was a French operative who preyed on the desperate and foolish to steal any kind of information that might be of use to the enemies of England. Langlais wasn't his real name, nor was he even French. He was a glorified highwayman who had run into luck with weak-minded aristocrats whom he never paid in the end.

Sophie had no qualms at all about proceeding with the plan to catch Lord Grey after learning how easily his treachery had been bought. What surprised her was how swiftly Nigel and his colleagues managed to locate Langlais and take him quietly into custody.

"Why did they not simply pluck him out of his bed like that before now?" she asked Jonathan as she stood by his side in his workshop the day before the engagement party, working madly to create the number of cakes that Lord Grey had requested for his sister's ball.

"Even the law has its limits," Jonathan told her. "Suspicion is one thing, but I'm sure Nigel felt it would have been beyond his reach to incarcerate the man without proof of his wrongdoings."

Whether Jonathan was right or not—and Sophie suspected he was—once Langlais was safe in prison, Nigel sent another Runner in disguise to take his place and to contact Lord Grey. Lord Grey, in turn, took the bait instantly, inviting the false French contact to Lady Charlotte's ball. Arrangements were made for the confidential shipping information to be hidden inside a particular design of éclair, which would be located on a secluded table in a room adjacent to the main refreshment room. A room which would be adorned with not one, but two living sugar sculptures who would sound the alarm and serve as witnesses the moment Lord Grey committed his treason.

"This is scandalous," Rebecca whispered as Jonathan offered her a hand up onto the table. She continued to clutch her robe tight long after Sophie had abandoned hers. "I cannot believe I am doing this."

"You said you wanted to help," Sophie laughed, receiving Rebecca as she stepped fully onto the table. "We can be the ones to catch Lord Grey in the act."

The only reason they wouldn't be catching Rebecca's

sister Mary in the act as well was that—in a fit of sisterly compassion—Rebecca had laced Mary's tea with ipecac that afternoon so that she would be too sick to attend the party. Although Sophie suspected the greater part of Rebecca's desire to keep her sister away from the party was so that Mary wouldn't find out how scandalous Rebecca had become.

"Like this?" Rebecca squeaked. She sat dubiously to the array of cushions that rested on the table.

"No," Sophie laughed, "like this." She lowered herself to recline on the cushions the way she and Jonathan had devised in the days before. Unlike her pose at the first banquet, her position for the ball would be more sleepy than erotic. Particularly because Rebecca would form part of the tableau with her.

"Are you certain?" Rebecca asked in a tiny voice.

"Lady Rebecca," Jonathan said in a respectful voice. "I am reluctant to push you into anything you are not ready for, but I need time to complete the illusion. You must decide whether to participate now."

Rebecca made an uncertain sound and bit her lip, then drew in a deep breath, squeezed her eyes closed, and peeled off her robe. She handed it to Jonathan without opening her eyes. "Ooh," she squealed. "This feels so bad."

Sophie laughed. "Which is precisely why it feels so good."

Rebecca took a few more, fast breaths, then opened her eyes long enough to orient herself on the table, then to sit in a position that mirrored Sophie's. Jonathan stepped forward and took hold of Rebecca's leg to position it the way they'd practiced the day before when they were both fully clothed. Rebecca gasped and tensed.

"Lady Rebecca, are you certain?" Jonathan asked. There was no need for Rebecca or Sophie to ask what he meant.

"You can do this," Sophie said, meeting and holding

Rebecca's gaze. "And remember, we will be wearing some of Honor's concealing masks with the eye holes filled in. There is no possible way either of us will be recognized."

"All right," Rebecca said as though attempting to bolster her courage. She shook her arms out to relax, then nodded for Jonathan to continue what he'd been doing. He moved her leg forward, placing it in front of one of Sophie's, then positioned her back leg between Sophie's calves so that their limbs appeared tangled. "Ooh," Rebecca squealed again. "This feels so strange. Especially after what that woman did to me."

Sophie couldn't stop herself from laughing. Glenda had treated Rebecca to the same, painful process with the wax and linen strips that Sophie had endured. She'd endured it a second time only that morning, but it hadn't been half as traumatic as before. "You'll get used to it," she promised. "And it has its advantages."

She sent a sultry, sidelong glance to Jonathan. He certainly enjoyed her smoothness, and she was convinced it heightened every sensation he provoked in her.

"No misbehaving here, my sweet," he scolded her with a smirk. "We have important work to do."

"You're right," Sophie agreed.

She took a deep breath and settled against the pillows that would need to keep her propped up until the trap was sprung on Lord Grey. Jonathan continued to arrange both her and Rebecca the way he needed them—backs slightly arched, breasts thrust forward, heads thrown back. Rebecca began to relax as Jonathan worked to the point where Sophie decided her dearest friend could be an accomplished vixen, if she put her mind to it. She had a slightly more voluptuous form than Sophie with comely curves and ample breasts. Peeking at her as Jonathan dusted Rebecca with sugar and placed sugar roses in a pattern on her belly made Sophie realize she'd never seen another woman quite so naked before. It was oddly alluring.

All the same, she cleared her throat and forced herself to focus on the moment at hand. They had spies to capture and ships to save. Jonathan concentrated deeply as he worked his sugar magic, so she would as well.

It was nearly an hour later before he finished.

"There," he said at last. "I'll fit your masks in place and make a few final adjustments, and then the trap will be set."

"I hope I can do this," Rebecca whispered. Sophie could feel her legs trembling.

"You'll do splendidly," Sophie said as Jonathan fit her mask over her face. "You'll see."

"If you think so," Rebecca sighed.

"There," Jonathan said at last, stepping back from the table. "You're ready. All we can do now is wait."

CHAPTER 9

Jonathan stepped back to survey his work, a buzz of excitement making him restless. In all the years he'd been creating cakes and sweets and sugar sculptures he'd never imagined they would be used for something as important as catching traitors to the crown. He'd hoped to make a name for himself and to be lauded by people of power and influence, and if their plan was a success, there was a good chance he would be praised.

He shook his head and laughed. Nothing in his life had ever followed the path he expected it to, and yet it had somehow managed to bring him the things that mattered all the same. He studied Sophie as she held perfectly still, a sensual confection, and the now familiar feeling of affection stirred within him. She'd blossomed in ways he wasn't sure she herself had noticed since their first meeting at Sebastian's wedding party. Confidence and sexuality radiated from her as she rested with her head back and her breasts thrust forward. Anxiety clearly rippled off of Rebecca—Jonathan hoped the nervous young woman would be able to play her part until the drama was over—but Sophie was in her element.

"I'm not certain this was a good idea," Nigel grumbled as he entered the room and stepped up to Jonathan's side. He spoke low enough that the women wouldn't hear him.

Jonathan turned to him with a frown that quickly melted to a teasing grin when he saw the way Nigel was staring at Rebecca. "It's a bit late to turn back now," he said.

Nigel rubbed a hand over the lower half of his face, continuing to drink in the sight of Rebecca's sugar-coated body. The evidence of his thoughts was a little too apparent in his tented breeches.

A moment later, he shook himself and said, "It's too sensual. One complaint by the wrong person—and the wrong persons are the entirety of the guest list—and they'll close off this room and send us all on our way."

"It's a risk," Jonathan admitted. "Which is why I've positioned the ladies less blatantly than I had Sophie at the banquet."

Nigel turned to him, one dark brow raised. "That is less blatant?"

In spite of the danger of the situation, Jonathan couldn't keep his laughter inside. His strong, sullen, giant of a friend was obviously unnerved by the simple sensuality of a society virgin attempting to be daring for the first time. And Jonathan was certain it was Rebecca that had Nigel so captivated, not Sophie.

"The way I have their legs, you can't stare straight at their cunts," Jonathan said, lowering his voice further as guests entered the room and exclaimed at the decorations. "And that much marzipan is as good as a chemise the way it covers them."

"Bullshit," Nigel growled. "You can see all of her tits. Her nipples alone—" He stood straighter and cleared his throat, then shifted his hips uncomfortably and tugged his jacket as though it had a chance of concealing things. "We need to take up our positions."

Nigel marched off to the far corner of the room, then stood mostly concealed behind a screen, his hands clasped in front of him, glaring at the preening, powdered guests who entered the room to gape at Sophie and Rebecca. Jonathan crossed to the other corner to stand guard behind a screen there.

The idea was that they would be on hand to pounce on Grey as soon as he attempted to pass on his secrets, but that neither of them would be noticeable at first glance. Of course, if Grey had a shred of intelligence at all, he would realize that Sophie and Rebecca were as capable of witnessing him and calling out his actions for what they were. But as of yet, Grey hadn't displayed any intelligence at all. That and the eyeless masks the women wore—coupled with their eerie stillness—gave the illusion that they were constructed of sugar as much as the cakes on offer around them.

"Look," one of the guests—a countess who had been invited to Jonathan's banquet—said to her companion in an excited voice. "The Delectable Tart. And she has a friend."

"Good heavens," the countess's companion gasped. "That's obscene."

"No, no," the countess corrected her. "The Delectable Tart is the talk of London. What a triumph for Lady Charlotte to secure her for this ball."

"Are you quite certain?" the companion asked. Several other people entered the room, murmuring and giggling as they viewed Sophie and Rebecca. "They look simply outrageous to me."

"Tush," the countess said, raising her voice and moving closer to the table. "It's no different than viewing the great works of Greek statuary on display at any museum in Europe."

From his position behind the screen, Jonathan could see that the countess had switched to addressing several other scandalized guests as though she were a scholar in one of those museums. His pulse raced for a completely unexpected reason. All it took was a few patrons—or patronesses—to deem his creations high art and a whole new set of doors would open to him. Their efforts to catch Grey might produce a whole different kind of fruit.

"Observe the classic beauty of their forms," the countess went on. "It is as if they are nymphs or muses from days of old. We are in the presence of great art."

"That's one word for it," a man standing near Jonathan's screen snorted.

"I can think of a few others," his friend said in return. "Either way, Grey is a bloody genius for hiring the Tart for his soiree."

"Was it Grey? Seems more like something Gosford would do," the first man said.

"Gosford would *do* anything," the second guffawed. "He's not too particular."

The men shared a laugh as they moved in to get a closer look at Sophie and Rebecca. Jonathan regretted not stationing himself closer to the ladies so that he could warn people not to touch them, as he had at the banquet. His unease grew as more and more people slipped into what was supposed to be a less traveled, secluded room. The curiosity of The Delectable Tart proved too much of a draw. If the stream of gawkers didn't lessen soon, Grey might not risk carrying out his plan to pass secrets at all.

"I won't have any of it, do you hear me?" Lady Charlotte's furious voice preceded her into the room. Jonathan stepped farther behind his screen at the first sight of the woman's furious, mottled face. She yelped angrily as she spotted the table where Sophie and Rebecca posed. "This is an outrage! Who did this? Who brought these whores into my house?"

Rebecca flinched and apparently began to lose her nerve, but Sophie remained perfectly motionless as guests fled the room in the wake of Lady Charlotte's fury. Jonathan was inches away from stepping out of his cover and attempting to diffuse the situation when Lord Gosford marched into the room.

"Charlotte, darling, what is the problem?" he asked, sidling up to his soon-to-be bride.

"I told you not to call me that," Lady Charlotte snapped. "And look." She flung her arm out at Sophie and Rebecca—who had resumed her pose but was shaking just enough to be noticeable.

"Good heavens," Gosford exclaimed in a reverent tone. "Grey hired The Delectable Tart? How magnificent."

"It's filthy," Lady Charlotte roared. "How could he? How could you stand there and gawp at such a display?"

"You have to admit, Charlotte, darling, the sight does inspire one to *amour*," Gosford said, lowering his tone to a lascivious purr and stepping closer to Lady Charlotte.

"I said don't call me—oh!"

Lady Charlotte shrieked as Gosford clamped a hand around her backside. She jumped away from him. "How dare you, sir?"

"I'm no sir, I'm your betrothed," Gosford chuckled. "And there's plenty more where that came from, eh, darling?"

He patted her backside a second time, sending Lady Charlotte into a mix of sound and expression that was something between growling and weeping.

"This is not how it was supposed to be," she lamented, fleeing from the room. "Not at all."

Gosford followed her, laughing. "Come on now, darling. We'll have fun enough on our wedding night."

Jonathan didn't know whether to feel sorry for Lady Charlotte or to laugh at the situation. One way or another, people got what they deserved in life, or so it seemed. The effect of Lord Gosford's teasing benefitted his own cause, though. After he and Lady Charlotte left, the room was empty and silent. It continued to be so for several minutes. Jonathan stepped halfway out from behind his screen to assess the situation.

Sophie hadn't moved a muscle, as if the entire incident had passed her by without notice. Rebecca's chest was heaving in relief—so much so that some of her decorations had cracked—but appeared to be settling herself and relaxing into her pose once more. Nigel poked his head out from his screen to look around as well. He wore a dark frown and looked ready to call the whole thing off.

But before he could say anything, the moment they'd been waiting for arrived. Lord Grey slipped into the room with furtive steps, glancing over his shoulder every three seconds. He didn't appear to see Jonathan or Nigel as they rushed behind their screens. He moved anxiously forward. As he reached the table where Sophie and Rebecca posed— both perfectly still—he reached a hand into his jacket pocket.

Jonathan held his breath. He prayed that Grey was as foolish and desperate as they needed him to be. He prayed that the Runner Nigel had arranged to play the part of Grey's new, French contact was right around the corner, and that Grey would be caught red-handed. He prayed that his father's shipping business would be able to continue uninterrupted. And most intensely of all, he prayed that Sophie would emerge from the ruse triumphant and that she would feel vindicated after her banishment from society.

Grey reached the table and drew a small roll of paper

from his jacket. He hunched in, peeking over his shoulder for a moment to be certain he was alone, then picked up one of several éclairs that were custom designed to tempt him.

A heartbeat later, Nigel's man marched into the room.

"Did you bring the secrets?" he asked Grey in an unconvincing French accent.

Gray gasped so hard he coughed, then spun to face the Runner. "Yes," he hissed. "Be quiet. No one can know what we're doing."

"And what are we doing?" the Runner asked.

Grey looked at him as though he were the dolt and handed him the éclair. "I've slipped the shipping register into this pastry. It details the route and intended cargo of a dozen ships on their way back from the orient. Waylay them and you will deal a crushing blow to British commerce. Now where's my money?"

Jonathan's jaw dropped. Grey was stupider than he ever could have imagined. He'd confessed to treason without the rest of them having to do a thing to draw it out of him. But Sophie went forward with their plan all the same.

"Spy," she shouted, springing out of her position and standing on the table. "Lord Grey is a spy for the French! Sound the alarm!"

Rebecca scrambled to her feet as well, and both Jonathan and Nigel leapt out from behind their screens. Lord Grey went instantly white, his eyes bulging and his mouth open in a silent scream.

"Lord James Grey," Nigel said, marching forward. "I arrest you in the name of the King on the charge of treason."

"You...but I didn't...you can't...." Grey gaped and floundered.

"We have all the proof we need right here," the Runner said, holding up the éclair, his attempt at an accent gone. "I trust this information is in your own hand?"

"Wait, I can explain," Grey said.

Instead of explaining, he broke into a run. He didn't make it more than a single step before Nigel captured him and wrestled his arms behind him.

At the same time, several guests poured into the room. They gaped at the scene unfolding in front of them—from Nigel wrestling Grey into submission to the Runner digging Grey's treasonous note out of the éclair to Sophie and Rebecca standing fully naked on the table. Sophie had removed her mask so that she could watch the scene as it unfolded, but Rebecca kept hers on, in spite of the eye holes being filled in, leaving her blind. She moved behind Sophie, attempting to conceal herself.

"Lord Grey is a spy," Sophie announced to the guests, who continued to pour into the room. "He has just been caught passing shipping information to the French."

The guests gasped in shock, staring at Grey instead of Sophie, in spite of her nakedness.

"I lost nearly thirty thousand pounds when a ship was taken by the French," one of the guests shouted.

"It is a betrayal of king and country," another said.

"Is there proof?" a third asked.

"There is," the Runner said, holding up the cream-coated note. "Enough for Lord Grey to hang."

"No," Lord Grey wailed and sagged against Nigel, no longer fighting his hold.

"No!" The shout was echoed by Lady Charlotte as she pushed her way through the increasing crowd in an attempt to reach her brother. "James, say this is not so. Say it is a misunderstanding." She glanced desperately around, laughing madly. "This must be part of the entertainment for the evening. Yes, that must be it. James, stop at once. It isn't funny anymore."

"It is not an entertainment," Nigel said. "Rob and I are

here with all the authority of the courts. Your brother has been the subject of an ongoing investigation into espionage and piracy. And based on the evidence we now have—as well as the witnesses to his confession just now—he will hang for this, my lady."

"No," Lady Charlotte cried. "No, this cannot be right."

"The Greys are spies?" someone in the crowd—which now filled the room, clogged the doorway, and spilled into the larger refreshment room—said.

"Treason," someone else said. The word was instantly repeated in rippling waves that spread from the room and out into the house.

"Get me out of here," one of the guests who had rushed into the room first and stood at the front of the crowd said. He turned and began pushing people out of the way in his efforts to leave. "I want nothing to do with a family of traitors."

"Neither do I," another guest said.

Within seconds, the tide of guests turned in the other direction and people pushed to get as far away from Grey and his sister as they could. If Jonathan's guess was correct, the entire Grey house would be empty within minutes, as if it had caught fire.

"No," Lady Charlotte repeated, far weaker and with almost no energy. "Come back. Come back. I am one of you. I am a diamond of the first water."

Her protests fell on deaf ears, and she collapsed, sinking to her knees, then bending forward to fold herself into a weeping, shivering ball.

Sophie climbed quickly off the table and went to her, kneeling beside her and slipping an arm around the odious woman's shoulders. "It will be all right," she said. "If you are strong, you will survive this and build a whole new life for yourself."

"Get away from me, you whore," Lady Charlotte shrieked, snapping up and pushing Sophie away. "Keep your filth away from me. You disgust me." She pushed herself to her feet and fled from the room.

Sophie stood with a sad sigh. She glanced to Jonathan with a look that said she'd tried her best.

"Harris and Verne are waiting outside," Rob, the Runner, told Nigel, reaching for Grey's limp arm. "We'll take this one to Newgate."

Grey didn't protest. He merely moaned like a petulant toddler and let Rob drag him from the room. As soon as they were gone, Jonathan moved to close the door.

"Is it over?" Rebecca asked, removing her mask and stepping down from the table.

"It is," Sophie told her with a wide grin. "We've won."

She skipped over to the table and hugged her friend tightly. In spite of everything, Jonathan's blood heated at the sight of the two naked women embracing each other.

"God help me," Nigel grumbled. "That's a sight I won't forget anytime soon."

The ladies seemed to have no idea how their intimacy stirred Jonathan and Nigel. Guilty as it made him feel, Jonathan regretted it when Sophie stepped away from Rebecca.

"We've won," she repeated, rushing to Jonathan and throwing herself in his arms.

That was an even more delicious treat. Jonathan kissed her soundly, tasting sugar and spice and the unique flavor that was Sophie. "I never could have done any of this without you."

He moved to kiss her again, but a knock sounded at the door, and a moment later, the countess who had compared Sophie and Rebecca to Greek art poked her head into the room.

"Oh," she exclaimed when she saw Sophie in Jonathan's arms. "It is true, then?"

Rebecca squeaked and leapt behind Nigel's massive body to hide.

"Your ladyship?" Jonathan asked, wondering if he should do the same for Sophie.

But no, Sophie stepped away from him and executed a perfect, gracious curtsy, bits of icing and sugar flowers crumbling off her naked body as she did. "Lady Stafford," she said with utmost respect.

Lady Stafford stared at her with wide eyes. "The Delectable Tart is Miss Sophie Barnes?" she asked stepping all the way into the room. "I never would have guessed."

"It is true, my lady," Sophie said. She straightened and faced the woman as though they were in Hyde Park and Sophie was fully clothed.

Lady Stafford swept an appreciative glance over Sophie's body, then cleared her throat. "I had to see for myself. Rumors are flying, after all. Lord Grey has been arrested for treason and will hang. Lady Charlotte has gone mad. And Miss Sophie Barnes is The Delectable Tart."

"All are true, my lady," Sophie confirmed with a nod.

"What an invigorating evening," Lady Stafford said, smiling. She turned to Jonathan. "And you are Mr. Jonathan Foster, are you not?"

"I am, your ladyship." Jonathan bowed to her.

"Might I ask, sir," she said, stepping closer to him. "Do you have a card?"

"A card, your ladyship?" Jonathan asked, hope rising within him.

"Yes," she continued. "I am a great admirer of your work." She glanced to Sophie with a sparkle in her eyes. "I should very much like to commission your unique brand of refreshment for a private celebration I will be hosting soon."

Jonathan fought to contain his grin. "I would be only too happy to cater to your celebration, your ladyship," he said. "But it must be with the understanding that certain items included within my display are not for sale or rental at any price, only for observation."

"Understood, Mr. Foster," Lady Stafford said with a knowing smile. She glanced to Sophie again with a sigh. "Though it is a pity. My husband and I would have enjoyed an interactive display."

Behind Nigel, Rebecca squeaked in shock. Sophie clapped a hand over her mouth to hide her giggle. Jonathan's heart felt lighter than air as he reached into the pocket of his jacket to take out a card for Lady Stafford.

"We are at your service, your ladyship," he said, handing over the card with a bow.

Lady Stafford took the card and tapped it to her lips, raking Jonathan with a glance. "Perhaps someday we could come to an arrangement that would be satisfactory to all," she said, winking then swaying out of the room.

"Bloody hell, man," Nigel grumbled, shaking his head. "I will never understand the upper classes."

Sophie burst into laughter, her face beet red. She rushed into Jonathan's arms once more. "Who could have imagined that such a short time after being utterly cast out by the *ton*, one of its most respected members would want me back in such a way?"

Jonathan considered that the question was best left unanswered. He kissed Sophie squarely on the lips, proud of the cool yet scandalous way she'd deported herself. "Let's go home," he said. "I've had enough of the nobility for one night."

"I'll make sure that Lady Rebecca makes it home safely," Nigel said, his face flushed and his look what could only be described as sheepish. He glanced over his shoulder, attempting to peek at Rebecca, but she shifted to one side. When he twisted to look over his other shoulder, she scooted out of his line of sight again. He finally gave up with a sigh. "I'll fetch your robe, my lady."

"Thank you," Rebecca said in a tiny voice.

"I'll get it. I should wear mine on the way home as well," Sophie said, skipping back to the table and lifting the cloth to retrieve both robes that had been stashed there.

Jonathan had the suspicion that if she could have gotten away with riding through the streets of London in the nude, she would have.

CHAPTER 10

*B*y the time they reached Jonathan's shop, Sophie had made up her mind that she was happier than she'd ever been in her life. It came as a shock to her.

"Can you imagine?" she asked as Jonathan handed her down from his carriage, then nodded to Freddy—who had worked tirelessly along with the Grey's staff throughout the party and was currently going above and beyond as driver—to drive the carriage on to the mews. "A year ago, I was at my wit's end, anxious about presenting a perfect image to the *ton* in order to secure a respectable marriage."

"And now?" Jonathan asked, laughter in his voice as he unlocked the front door of the shop and reached for her hand to lead her quickly inside.

No doubt the urgency of his gesture was because she wore nothing but a silk robe and slippers. In her defense, beneath the robe her skin was so sticky with sugar and icing that it would have been a Herculean feat to don the layers of clothing society dictated as civilized. Not that she minded. Sophie had rather come to enjoy walking about in the altogether of late.

She expanded on that thought by answering Jonathan's question with, "Now I am excessively happy being the most scandalous, most gossiped about woman in London." She added a happy sigh to her pronouncement as Jonathan escorted her through the darkened shop to the stairs and up to his living quarters.

Jonathan shook his head, a broad, proud smile making him appear both alluring and supportive. "As long as you are fully cognizant of how dangerous your tastes have become," he said.

"Dangerous?" Sophie arched one eyebrow teasingly as they entered the sitting room attached to Jonathan's bedroom.

Jonathan paused and turned to her, a frank look taking the place of his amusement. "If you intend to continue along this path, to continue to work with me and offer your body as an object to be admired and craved by all sorts, you will have to accept that there will be men who may try to take what you perceive to offer, by force if necessary."

"But they won't lay a finger on me," Sophie said with absolute sincerity. When Jonathan fixed her with a flat look that hinted he thought she was being naïve, she rushed on with, "They won't lay a finger on me because you will be by my side at every moment. I will be your muse and your creation and you will be my champion and protector." That vision of the future filled her with so much joy that she burst into a smile that could only be called silly and stepped into him, throwing her arms around his shoulders.

He closed his arms around her and kissed her, but it was only a short kiss. "You will never be accepted in polite society again if you choose to do this," he said, his expression full of concern.

"I was never going to be accepted into society again regardless," she said with all due seriousness.

Jonathan tilted his head to the side and made a sound of consideration. "Not necessarily. It was Lady Charlotte who caused your sisters to be banished, was it not?"

"It was."

"After tonight, I believe Lady Charlotte's day in the sun has come to an end. Even if Gosford goes through with the wedding—and laws and standards aside, it is conceivable that he may attempt to wiggle out of it—I doubt her ladyship will be able to show her face in London again. And if that is the case, the fortunes of you and your sisters may be restored."

"Perhaps." Sophie shrugged, resting her weight against him and enjoying the feeling of his strong chest against her curves. "Although my identity was revealed tonight. I am now damned on my own merits. And I doubt Honor would ever be accepted, having married a tradesman. And Verity would rather eat mud than rejoin the circles of the *beau monde*."

"What about you?" he asked, his voice a deep purr, his hands sliding down to cup her backside. "What do you want?"

So many wicked things sprung to Sophie's mind that she could only shiver and suck in a breath in reply. She wanted to enjoy fame as The Delectable Tart and all that came with it as long as possible. But more than that, she wanted to feel Jonathan's arms around her and his cock deep inside of her as often as possible. She wanted to lose herself in carnal bliss on a nightly basis and let Jonathan use her body in every way he could imagine until he was sated and happy. And beyond that, she wanted to watch herself grow round with his children and cradle his babies in her arm.

But instead of answering any of those things, she stepped back with a coy shrug and a mysterious, teasing smile. "At

THE DELECTABLE TART

this moment, what I would like more than anything else is a bath. I'm rather sticky, you see."

"I wager you are, my sweet," he said in a deep voice, raking her with a devilish grin that implied a stickiness not born of sugar. "I should bathe you with my tongue."

A thrill of desire thrummed through Sophie, reverberating in her sex, but she laughed. "Perhaps an hour ago, but at the present time I do not recommend it." She sniffed herself and made a face.

Jonathan joined her laughter. "I'll fetch the tub if you help bring water up."

Drawing a bath so late at night and being forced not only to cart bucket after bucket of water up a flight of stairs, but heating it over the fireplace in the front room of Jonathan's bedroom suite was the least romantic thing either of them could have done just then. It made Sophie even stickier and less savory than she'd been at the start. But it all seemed worth the effort when she finally shed her robe and sank into the lukewarm water.

"Not the most ideal conditions for a bath," she said as she squeezed the sponge over her shoulders to begin the cleansing process, "but necessary."

"It may be necessary," Jonathan said, pulling off his boots and shrugging out of his shirt, "but I believe we can still make it enjoyable."

In nothing but his breeches, he walked to the side of the tub and knelt, then took the sponge from Sophie. She was still too much of a mess to forego the bath entirely in favor of either climbing out of the tub to remove his breeches and play with what she revealed or to coax him into the tub with her, but it didn't seem to matter. Jonathan filled the sponge with water and squeezed it out over her sugary skin until the decorations he'd taken so much time to create began to wash away.

"Your body is beautiful," he said, switching to washing her back and arms with more purposeful strokes. "I don't think I could ever get enough of it."

Sophie beamed at the compliment. She let him move her arms and then her torso how he wanted in order to clean her the same way she let him pose her as a decoration. "My body will change, you know," she said. "All things change."

He shook his head. "It doesn't matter. You will still be the pinnacle of perfection to me."

She had a hard time not giggling, especially as he scooted down a bit in order to better bathe her front. "With all these sweets, I could grow fat in no time."

He scrubbed and teased her breasts in a way that was both careful and erotic. "It wouldn't matter," he said. "I would love you all the same."

Sophie sucked in a breath, her eyes popping wide. A moment later, Jonathan seemed to understand what he'd said. A flush warmed his cheeks and a smile spread across his lips.

"I'm not taking it back," he said, dragging the sponge down her stomach, into the water, then along one leg. "I said I love you, and I do. I'm proud to admit it."

"Even though we've only known each other for a few short weeks?" she asked, her heart racing in her chest.

"A few weeks or a lifetime," Jonathan said, switching to scrub her other leg. "When that little bastard, Cupid, aims his arrows, time becomes irrelevant."

Sophie laughed. She loved the way Jonathan said such scandalous things with a glint in his eyes. She loved how he managed to be romantic and sentimental while sounding crass and teasing. She could see in his eyes that the words he chose were nowhere near as important as the emotion behind them. And two could play at that game.

"How would you like a wet, slippery, sweet woman in your bed?" she asked, one eyebrow arched.

"I would like that immensely," he said with a growl.

He tossed the sponge aside and lifted Sophie out of the tub in one, strong swoop. As soon as her feet touched the ground, sugary water sluicing everywhere, she leaned into him, wrapping her arms around him. Jonathan didn't hesitate. He clasped her tightly, one hand squeezing her backside and the other spreading across her back. Sophie ground against his pronounced erection as he kissed her, claiming her with his lips and tongue in a way that marked her undeniably as his.

"You're still sweet," he murmured, kissing her chin and licking the water from her neck. She arched back to give him more of herself.

"I suspect it will take a series of baths to wash away all of the sugar," she said.

Her words ended in a gasp as he closed a hand around her breast and lifted it to meet his mouth. He teased her with his lips and teeth, swirled his tongue around her nipple and licked until it formed a hard, needy point, then sucked in a way that left her moaning. The heat and ache in her sex flared.

"Delicious," he sighed, straightening and capturing her mouth once more. "A tart I could feast on for the rest of my life."

Sophie laughed and ran her hands across his damp chest and down to the fastening of his breeches. "I know what I could feast on for the rest of my life."

She made quick work of the buttons of his breeches, cradling the hard length of his cock as the garment dropped loosely around his thighs. Jonathan hummed in appreciation, a dark fire in his eyes. Sophie still had much to learn when it came to pleasuring him, but she'd discovered how much he liked when she stroked him from balls to tip, paying special attention to the ridge around his tip and the slit at the end.

"I wouldn't call that feasting," he said in a rough voice, his eyes teasing.

"Nor would I," she said, acknowledging the subtle command by wetting her lips in anticipation.

She lowered herself to her knees as he stepped back to lean against the frame of the sliding doors that separated his bedroom from the sitting room. Her body tingled in expectation of the pleasure she was about to give him, and her heart skipped in her chest. She helped him step out of his breeches, then slid her hands up his thighs with an appreciative sound and gazed up at him with a look that was both submissive and excited. He rewarded her with an expression of such carnal approval that it made her want to play the submissive role even more. How curious it was that pretending to be at his mercy made her feel so powerful.

She grasped his cock gently, sliding her hand along its length a few times before bringing it to her mouth so that she could kiss and lick his tip. She felt him tense and hold his breath as she closed her lips around his head, teasing it with her tongue in prelude to everything that came next. Her skill had increased tenfold since their first night together, and when she bore down on him, she was able to swallow him deeply.

"My sweet," he gasped, fisting both hands in her hair as she drew him in so deep she was in danger of choking.

She drew him out slowly, then swallowed him again, setting a slow, steady rhythm that she hoped was driving him wild with desire. Her own body responded to his heat and girth filling her mouth. Her breasts begged to be fondled and her sex wept and ached to the point where she wasn't certain if it was water slipping down her thigh or her own moisture. She focused on his cock sliding in and out of her mouth, allowing him to take control and set the pace. He was desperate, eager, and greedy, breathing fast. One minute he tilted his head back as he reveled in the sensation of her mouth taking more and more of him, and the next he glanced down, no doubt watching his thickness sliding in and out of her lips.

"I can't," he panted, his grip on her hair tightening. "Good God, you're a siren. I can't...I can't—"

His panted words were cut off with a cry as his seed shot to the back of her throat. Sophie's eyes went wide and she swallowed on instinct. He'd never lost control that way before, but to her surprise she liked it. She'd made him spend in her throat. She'd been so desirable that he couldn't contain himself.

She pulled back, catching her breath and feeling more erotically alive than she ever had, especially when she caught sight of Jonathan sagging, sated, against the doorframe. Let the pristine ladies of the *ton* say what they would and faint in horror at the sight of her draped across a table of sweets. There was no power on earth as intoxicating as bringing a man to his knees with desire.

However, she had needs as well, and denial was only alluring if there was a promise of release.

"You've left me at a disadvantage, sir," she said, resting a hand on his chest. His heart thumped wildly. "You have found your release, but I am still tormented." She took a backward step toward his bed, brushing a hand over her breast. "Whatever shall I do?"

"You will let me love you," he said, pushing away from the doorframe and following her, his energy renewing.

As much as she longed to find some sort of coy or clever reply, all she could manage was a giggle as the back of her legs hit the edge of his bed. She tumbled back, balancing herself on her elbows and spreading her legs in invitation.

Jonathan didn't need much encouragement to advance on her, lifting her as he reached the bed and splaying her further across the covers. He climbed over her, sliding his muscular body along hers in a way that left her sighing for more.

"I'm sorry," he said, kissing her forehead and cheeks, and then her mouth. "Forgive me for coming so quickly, but you are more than I can handle sometimes."

"I see only one solution to the problem," she said, lifting her knees so that his half-engorged staff rested in the cradle of her hips. She slipped her arms around his sides to dig her fingertips into his back.

"What is your solution?" he asked, moving his hips against her wet opening without penetrating her, as though intent on working his cock back to a rock-hard state. He rubbed her clitoris in the process, though not intensely enough to send her over the edge. "Shall I ravish you until you scream with pleasure and weep my name?"

Sophie hummed at the thought, her smile perfectly naughty. "Yes, please. But that is not the solution I had in mind."

"It's not?" He paused, lifting himself so that he could gaze down at her with a combination of desire and curiosity.

"No, I think there's only one true solution to the problem of us being so overwhelmed with each other that we unravel too soon," she said, arching into him.

"And that is?" he prompted.

She slipped one hand between them, stroking his cock to gauge how close he was to being ready to fuck her. Her body was primed and ready and aching to feel him inside of her, filling and taking what he wanted. He reacted in kind by closing a hand around one of her breasts and teasing her nipple with his thumb. The whole thing was so intensely erotic that she thought she would burst.

"It's obvious, isn't it?" she gasped, wriggling her hips and

THE DELECTABLE TART

guiding him to her entrance. He pressed into her, but only by an inch—enough to leave her gasping for more.

"Now you're simply teasing me," he said, doing exactly the same to her by penetrating her only enough to leave her whimpering for more.

"Marry me," she gasped, bearing down on him to draw him in farther. "Marry me so that I am in your bed every night. I want to be yours in every way, always."

The shock that was clear in his eyes was not enough to stop him from sinking fully into her. Sophie let out a soft cry and arched her back as he filled her. But he stopped when he was buried deep, looking down at her in wonder.

"You want to be my wife?" he asked, sounding breathless and confused.

"Dear God, yes," she said, writhing under him to cause just enough friction as he attempted to stay planted where he was inside of her.

"Even though I am a humble confectioner and the son of a slave?" he asked, something deeper than surprise spreading through his expression.

"You are an artist," she gasped, giving up hope that he could be pushed into moving within her and setting off the spark that would cause her body to burst into flame at last. "You are the son of a nobleman and a fine businessman to boot."

He began to move, almost as though he couldn't hold still a moment longer. "Marriage to me would be fodder for gossip for years to come," he said, his voice strained with passion.

"I don't care," she said with abandon, fast approaching the point where she wouldn't be capable of speech or thought. "I love you. So very much. I am better with you than I could ever be without."

He groaned, though whether from carnal satisfaction or

heartfelt emotion, Sophie couldn't tell. "My sweet," he rumbled, shifting slightly so that he could pound into her with the speed and force that she loved. "I love you," he went on, his words uttered in primal grunts. "With everything I have. But I'll only marry you if you scream my name when you come."

Sophie gasped, then burst into something that was part laughter and part moans of pleasure. He was teasing her again, igniting her heart as his body joined with hers. He must have known full well that the relentless, possessive way he was fucking her would have her crying out his name whether she tried to or not.

She teetered on the edge before she knew it. "Oh," she mewled. "It's close, it's so close. It's—Jonathan!" She shouted his name with the full force of passion as her body throbbed into release.

"Yes," he growled, the word dissolving into a roar as her cunny squeezed him. "Yes, my sweet."

His body tensed as he came. Warmth spread through Sophie, but not simply because of his seed spilling into her. He was hers, body and soul, and she was his. He was saying yes to sharing a life with her, whatever wildness that life contained. The world could judge them as harshly as it liked. As long as they had each other, Sophie would be the proudest, happiest woman on earth.

EPILOGUE

Sophie would have given anything to be the centerpiece of her own wedding banquet, but the practicalities of being a bride surrounded by family and friends and the requirements of lying on a table filled with cakes and sweets, coated in sugar and fully on display, simply did not go together.

"I will be the crowning glory of Jonathan's display in a fortnight, when he provides his pastries for Lord Pennington's rout," she told Verity, Honor, and Rebecca as they conversed in the center of a room filled with colorful and interesting wedding guests.

"Who would have thought that our little Sophie would become the talk of London?" Verity asked, beaming with pride.

"Well, the talk of a certain portion of London," Honor added in a more cautious tone.

"All of London is talking about her," Verity said, shaking her head. "Although only half of the talk is worth listening to."

Sophie laughed, feeling a bit guilty for doing so. She shouldn't have taken so much pride in gaining the sort of notoriety she had over the past few months as Jonathan's canvas. The so-called polite members of the *ton* had taken to averting their eyes when she passed them on the street, although she was well aware that a goodly portion of those people also begged, borrowed, or stole in order to obtain an invitation to a party where they knew she would be on display. As it often did, notoriety had made her a celebrity.

"The talk will die down soon enough," Sophie admitted with a sigh, lowering her hand to her stomach. "Though Jonathan and I intend to push the boundaries of what society will accept for as long as possible. I should think an *enceinte* centerpiece would cause quite a stir."

"You wouldn't," Rebecca gasped, her eyes round.

"Of course she would," Verity laughed, resting a hand on the bump that proclaimed her own fertile condition. "For I do believe that Sophie is the most daring of us all."

"She is," Honor agreed, keeping more to protocol by not acknowledging her own growing stomach, though it was as obvious as Verity's. "I may be wicked beyond all possible telling in private, but I prefer to keep that wickedness between me and my husband." She glanced across the room to where Sebastian was congratulating Jonathan along with Thomas and a few of their friends.

"You may have a point," Verity said, her cheeks turning pink when Thomas caught her studying him and winked. "There are quite a few things I would do in private that I wouldn't care to share."

"There are things I choose to keep private as well," Sophie argued, recalling the way she'd ridden Jonathan that morning as he fondled her swelling breasts. "But there are others that I do not mind displaying to the public as well," she finished with a naughty smile and a laugh.

Her sisters laughed with her, but Rebecca continued to look flabbergasted. "I nearly expired the night Lord Grey was taken away," she said in somber tones. "All those people looking at me?" She shivered.

"I can think of one gentleman in particular who enjoyed looking at you," Sophie said with a teasing wink. She nodded across the room to where Nigel was attempting—and failing—to engage Madison in conversation. She peeked at Rebecca, laughing once more when her friend turned a deep shade of red. "He saw you home that evening, did he not?"

"He did," Rebecca squeaked.

"And?" Verity asked, her eyes aglow with mischief.

"And I am not half as brave as the lot of you," Rebecca said in a small voice.

"Perhaps you could be, under the right circumstances," Honor joined in the teasing.

Rebecca let out a sigh and shook her head. "Mama is determined to marry me off to a gentleman of the highest distinction, now that Mary's chances have been ruined."

Sophie hummed in sympathy and squeezed her friend's hand. Even though she had avoided being implicated in Lord Grey's treason by staying home from Lady Charlotte's engagement party, Lady Mary had been tarnished by her close association with the Greys all the same. It did not help her cause that certain letters and diaries penned by Mary had circulated among the ladies of the *ton*. Thanks to Rebecca, of course. And even though Mary was in no danger of hanging—unlike Lord Grey, whose upcoming trial was widely known to be a mere formality before the noose was fitted—it seemed strangely fitting that she would leave England for the island of Bermuda as a traveling companion of the recently-jilted Lady Charlotte. Like Bonaparte, neither woman was expected to ever return from their island exile.

"I'm sure with time your parents will recover from the

events of the season," Sophie said, giving Rebecca's hand a final squeeze. "You have three fine, upstanding brothers to maintain your family's fortunes, and if your tastes did incline toward a more unconventional path, given time I'm quite certain you could begin a whole new, thoroughly exciting life."

Rebecca chewed her lip, stealing a glance at Nigel, then snapping to face Sophie once more the moment Nigel noticed her staring. "It's best not to think about it," she whispered.

"If you do think about it," Sophie said, "and if you would like any advice, you have three thoroughly debauched jades standing by your side. I dare say that any of us would fill your head with so much information that you would throw yourself at Mr. Kent simply for relief."

Verity and Honor laughed, nodding in agreement. Rebecca laughed as well, but she looked as though she might faint at any moment. Sophie knew something of how she felt. She'd been shocked by the lives her sisters had chosen at first. Now she knew that happiness was most certainly possible in that sort of life, even if respectability and acceptance by polite society weren't. She was highly pleased with her choices, though.

When Jonathan broke away from Sebastian and Thomas and headed across the room toward her, Sophie took her leave of Rebecca and her sisters and went to meet him.

"You look more beautiful with every passing day," he said as he met her near a window that looked out onto Thomas's garden.

"I'm certain it is merely the halo one acquires when one is expecting," she said, slipping comfortably into his arms in spite of their guests.

"You? Wearing a halo?" he teased her, lowering a hand to squeeze her backside.

"It is only borrowed, I can assure you," she laughed.

He leaned in to kiss her, but as he straightened, his expression grew more serious. "Can you ever forgive me for landing you in this condition before the vows were spoken?" he asked.

Sophie laughed at his earnestness. "We've already broken the rules a hundred times over. I see no need to hold on to any regrets as to when our family began, only the joy I cannot describe because it has begun."

"My sweet," Jonathan said, sultrier than he should have at a party. He closed his arms more tightly around her and kissed her gently. "You've made me the happiest man alive simply by being the wild, wanton, imaginative woman you are."

"And we will both continue to be happy for as long as we live," she replied, "because we belong to each other."

૭ቈ

I HOPE YOU HAVE ENJOYED SOPHIE AND JONATHAN'S SILLY, sexy, sticky story! I have to confess that I wasn't sure I wanted Jonathan to be the character he ended up being. But this is a case where the character absolutely demanded to be written the way he wanted to be, regardless of my reservations.

The sugar trade in the late 18th and early 19th century was wildly controversial and remains so to this day. Men made massive fortunes throughout Europe off of the relatively new commodity. Sugar and sweets were in demand like they'd never been before. Pastry chefs like Marie-Antoine Carême —who was very much a real person and was the father of many of the modern pastry-making techniques we take for granted today—became celebrities and were feted throughout the royal courts of Europe. Almost all of those first celebrity chefs came from the poorest classes. Many had formerly worked as servants in the households of the French nobility, and after their masters were dragged to the guillotine, they were forced to find a way to use their skills to support themselves. So on the one hand, it is perfectly accurate that a man like Jonathan could have risen up from obscurity to become a celebrity.

On the other hand, the sugar trade relied on slave labor. Slave conditions on Caribbean sugar plantations were some of the most horrible the world has known. That being said, plantation owners often had entire families with slaves or former slaves, and quite often they would set their biracial children up in what they considered normal lives…provided they looked more like their European parent. While I didn't go into this in great detail, in my mind Jonathan was chosen from among his brothers to set up an office for his father's business in London because he was the one who could "pass" most easily. Which is where the moral conundrum of everything that Jonathan did and was—and everything that the real-life people who lived the sort of life Jonathan did—lives that most definitely existed but that history has frequently attempted to erase—lies. Jonathan's wealth and success were absolutely built on the enslavement of his relatives. Which is why I was super hesitant to write him the way he wanted to be written. Because this story is supposed to be a comedy.

In the end, I decided it was more important to show the variety of people who inhabited Regency London than it was to delve into the darker side of pre-abolition politics and economies. I hope you can forgive me for only telling part of the story.

AND FOR THOSE OF YOU WHO ARE CURIOUS ABOUT WHAT COULD

happen between Rebecca and Nigel, well, keep your eyes peeled and sign up for my newsletter so that you can be alerted when the next exciting books are released!

Click here for a complete list of other works by Merry Farmer.

ABOUT THE AUTHOR

I hope you have enjoyed *The Delectable Tart*. If you'd like to be the first to learn about when new books in the series come out and more, please sign up for my newsletter here: http://eepurl.com/cbaVMH And remember, Read it, Review it, Share it! For a complete list of works by Merry Farmer with links, please visit http://wp.me/P5ttjb-14F.

Merry Farmer is an award-winning novelist who lives in suburban Philadelphia with her cats, Torpedo, her grumpy old man, and Justine, her hyperactive new baby. She has been writing since she was ten years old and realized one day that she didn't have to wait for the teacher to assign a creative writing project to write something. It was the best day of her life. She then went on to earn not one but two degrees in History so that she would always have something to write about. Her books have reached the Top 100 at Amazon, iBooks, and Barnes & Noble, and have been named finalists in the prestigious RONE and Rom Com Reader's Crown awards.

ACKNOWLEDGMENTS

I owe a huge debt of gratitude to my awesome beta-readers, Caroline Lee and Jolene Stewart, for their suggestions and advice. And double thanks to Julie Tague, for being a truly excellent editor and assistant! Thanks also to the members of the Historical Harlots Facebook Group, who provide me with all sorts of inspiration!

Click here for a complete list of other works by Merry Farmer.

Printed in Great Britain
by Amazon